D1645332

also by
Eda Lord

A MATTER OF CHOOSING
CHILDSPLAY

extenuating
circumstances

EDA LORD

extenuating circumstances

Hodder and Stoughton
London Sydney Auckland Toronto

01719066

254152325

ORMSKIRK

Copyright © 1971 by Eda Lord. First printed in Great Britain 1972.
ISBN 0 340 16288 0. Reproduced from the original setting by arrangement
with Alfred A. Knopf, New York. All rights reserved. No part of this
publication may be reproduced or transmitted in any form or by any
means, electronic or mechanical, including photocopy, recording, or any
information storage and retrieval system, without permission in writing
from the publisher. Printed in Great Britain for Hodder and Stoughton
Limited, St. Paul's House, Warwick Lane, London EC4P 4AH by
Compton Printing Ltd., London and Aylesbury.

To
   Darsie Gillie

extenuating circumstances

chapter
one

Day after day in June 1940 the sun shone, the sea spar-
kled, the sun poured down on the empty beaches and on
the harbor at Cannes with its yachts and small craft bat-
tened down and shrouded as for winter.

The Croisette was black with the fusty attire from
the North: the homeless in their hot Sunday best, sweat-
ing, pushing, shoving in the scramble to find a place to
sleep and something to eat. Shops were shuttered blind
and padlocked, or they gaped bare. Gutted.

The refugees kept on the move because there was no
place to stop. Benches and cafés were packed, packed to
sit out the day. Those who were in possession of a seat
looked about them sullen, dazed, suspicious. The man
at the next table . . . his clothes did not look slept in. He
had shaved. Why was he better off? Whom did he pay on
the side? Where in heaven's name would all this end?
They stared at the sea and that seemed the answer. It was
the obstacle which had stopped them.

Suddenly, unbelievably, salvation came. Out of the

blue, over the air, on the wireless. Pétain, that legendary figure from the past, spoke to the nation. He was negotiating for an armistice. Those who heard him said, "It is another German trick, and not good enough this time. The voice has too much quaver, it is too senile."

The recorded speech was repeated the next day. Somehow, overnight, the entire French nation had heard, found itself convinced, and was about-face: *The Hero of Verdun is saving us for a second time. Henceforth, European affairs will be settled by Europe. England deserted us at Dunkirk.*

Presto-chango, England was the enemy.

The English, broadly speaking, were gone from Cannes, but Letty Innes-Gore had not budged.

One by one and in groups Letty had watched her friends leave, and not one of them was able to persuade her to go along, not even John and Laura Winslow. Stubborn as a mule, John called her. Laura said, "You have some high-falutin idea of sticking by the ship. Mark my words, you're on the wrong boat."

Letty shook her head.

Neither she nor the Winslows had the slightest idea that she was in a serious state of shock. Letty gave no outward sign that she was not her usual self. She suggested going with them to Marseilles so that she could drive John's Bentley back home and garage it. There was just enough petrol for that. She promised to keep an eye on their house and grounds and, above all, to watch over John's collection of pictures. All this they discussed in the

4

car. The chance to get to England on an old coaling boat had presented itself at the last minute. There had been no time for arrangements. As they bumped over tram tracks and rumbled through the outskirts of Marseilles, John admitted that Letty's decision to stay did ease his mind about the pictures. He'd written out a check, he said, for the balance of his account in France—francs were of no further use to him—and she'd find it in his jacket pocket, on her side. Letty would not take it until he said, "If you don't, the Germans or their lackeys will get it."

The coaling boat was small, all too obviously a tight squeeze for the passengers massed at the foot of the gangplank. Ship's officers stood blocking the way. After some time it was announced by loudspeaker that each person who came aboard was limited to one suitcase only. No dogs or pets of any sort would be allowed. The crowd broke apart to disgorge a large chunk, people with dogs on leashes.

John picked out the two overnight cases from their luggage. "We have a chance if we go now," he said. They embraced Letty, and John nodded toward the tangle of sniffing, straining dogs. "Scram now, if you want to keep your sanity."

The Winslow house was a few hundred yards up the hill from Letty's. She went up there in the mornings, at first to unpack the trunks, then to cover the furniture. There were the hundred and one details of shutting up a house. In John's desk, where he told her they would be, she found the insurance papers for the pictures—a Swiss company, and good till the end of the year—"Good, my foot," she said to herself. At least it was a list, an inventory with valuation: one Bonnard, one Braque, one Degas, three Matisses, one Monet, two Picassos, and three Renoirs. She went to each in turn and stared at it rather malevolently. Not one of them was small and John had said it was better for them not to be crated, not to be taken off to a damp cellar or a hot attic. He wanted them left hanging. The amount they were valued at made Letty's heart stop. What if someone broke in at night?

She began to sleep badly. At first light she would rush up to look round and reassure herself. It was not long before refugees started breaking into abandoned villas or into any empty house. So Letty opened the shutters every morning to give a lived-in appearance. She even uncovered the furniture on the ground floor. Very soon she was going down to her own house only to make the bed and cook. She was too nervous to sit at home doing nothing. There was nothing to do because there was nothing to do it with, no soap or polish or thread. She would have to be careful with her brooms and mops. Up at the big house at least she felt useful. Her presence was useful. She walked about outside under the trees or sat in a deck chair holding a book.

Then, one morning when she went up to open the shutters, she heard voices from the back garden. She pushed a shutter the merest crack. A family was camping under the mulberry tree. Blankets were spread out and the man was lighting a fire of twigs.

Letty knew the temper of refugees. She slipped out of the front door and down through the trees to the gate. She went straight on down to the harbor. The ship chandler shop was shuttered, but she kept her finger on the bell because she knew that Frank slept there. Frank Morin was the French Canadian who looked after John's boat. She hadn't thought of Frank until she'd heard those voices. He came to the door half-asleep, pulling down his jersey. But the moment Letty told him about the campers, he locked his shop and was on his way up the hill with her.

"The trouble is," he said, "you can't leave a house like that empty. I'd sleep there myself if it weren't for the stuff in my shop."

"I'll move," said Letty. "There's nothing in my house worth stealing."

Frank faced the refugees alone. Letty's accent was against her. She went into the house to bang open the shutters and shake rugs, anything to give the impression of a household astir. Afterwards Frank said, "They did think it was empty. I rushed them while they were off-balance. Told them to be quick because I was holding back the dogs from their morning run."

"How did they get in?"

"The way they went, I imagine. Up an olive tree and along a branch which hung over the wall. I waited until I heard their car start."

Frank went off to the garage in search of a saw, and Letty went to her house to get something for breakfast. As they were sitting over the steaming cups, faintly reminiscent of coffee, Frank said, "What about the pictures? Did he get them out?"

"It was too late."

He turned over that bit of news in silence. Then he

stood up, leaning on the back of the chair. "The only thing to do now," he said, "is to go the rounds of the wall and lop off all overhanging branches." The wall itself was high enough to take care of the ordinary customer. He started off and turned back. "Why don't you ask someone to come in with you? The house is too large for one person, and it is isolated."

Her face reddened. "My French friends and I . . . are no longer on speaking terms."

He nodded. It was what he had expected. "If you pack your cases, I'll bring them up later. I've got a cart below."

Letty stood in her kitchen and looked round her. She hated leaving her house, and being obliged to do so angered her. She lashed out at fate. You thought you could get away with it, didn't you, by staying? You refused to go to England because you couldn't bear to leave your house. Haven't you learned yet that the more you cling to something, the more certain it is to be taken away?

She set to work packing stores and oddments in market baskets. Back and forth, up and down the hill, carrying not much at one time, she moved out of her house. The monotony of what she was doing took over and calmed her. Because every object she handled reminded her of the past, her thoughts fell in that direction. Take her monomania for France. That is what had shaped her life. Quite naturally so. She was fourteen when the 1914 war broke out, a receptive age, and she had swallowed whole every scrap of propaganda. From that time onward France was the embodiment of courage, honor, and glory. As black and white as that: the French could do no wrong.

"*Oh, can't they?*" she said aloud. In these last months they had smashed the very foundations of her belief. What was left was smoking rubble. Would she ever be able to clear it away? So much was buried under it. Her beloved brother who had been killed in France in 1917. And she might as well include her husband; he had been so terribly wounded. She had married her brother's hero and fellow-officer, Tom Innes-Gore. Tom had been invalided out of the regular army and told that his one chance to live was to go to a warm sunny climate, and so they had chosen the South of France. He died in the winter of 1931, the year the pound fell. Letty had had to use up a good deal of capital to pay the doctors and nurses and hospital expenses. Letty's one idea, her one hope (indeed determination), was to go on living in France. When the affairs were settled, she found that it was just possible. She owned the house and she could manage on the reduced income and on her pension as an officer's widow.

Nursing Tom year after year had been a rigid confinement. For a few short weeks she was happy in her new freedom. Then Laura Winslow had sought her out. She hadn't seen Laura since they had been at boarding school together. Laura approached her as though it had been yesterday. She bullied her as she had always done, and Letty weakly complied as she used to do in the past. Laura said that she and John would not allow Letty to bury herself in grief. John would take Letty sailing whenever he went out; it would be a kindness on Letty's part to go, she said, because she herself couldn't stand the motion.

Letty took to sailing like a duck to water and they were out almost every day. She began to be fond of John and she had always liked Laura. What irritated her was that Laura had no half-measures. She insisted that Letty be present at all their evening parties. Trying to scrape together the proper clothes was a maddening business and it was a drain on her finances. She got by. Just. With a hangover of poor-relation anxiety. If only it could have been left to her own decision. She might well have enjoyed a party from time to time. Although that situation changed entirely with the war, there was a residue of the old feeling left. So that when the Winslows decided to go to England, Letty's first emotion was relief. She would be on her own. That was before she had time to think.

She stared up at the big gate as she came near. The Winslows might be gone but they still had their fingers on her life. Frank opened the gate and held out his hand for her load. He scolded her for carrying so much.

"You have finished your fortress?" she said to change the subject and because she wondered at some complacency in his manner.

"I've made a discovery," he said. "A door in the back wall, overgrown with ivy and brambles. Did you know? Is there a key?"

Letty had never heard of it but she led him into the office where John kept all his keys hanging on a board. They found one marked "back wall" and Letty, astonished by Frank's eagerness, asked why it was important.

"An escape hatch," he said. "Come on."

He cut away the brambles and Letty watched. "Takes me back to the games we used to play," she said. "Bandits and robbers, red Indians."

"You are on the right track," he said, and the lock gave under his efforts. Opposite was a high wall like theirs and, in between, a narrow rocky way. "It could be a rain channel and lead nowhere," he said.

They slithered down to a right-angle turn at the end of John's wall. Now the other side was backed by houses and the way underfoot was cobbled. Another sharp corner and Frank said, "A short cut. We're in the old town. Let's have a drink at the shop."

He took Letty into the machine shop at the back and poured out two tumblers of red wine. He placed the key on the table between them. He asked if he might have a second one cut, because then, he said, he could be with her in five minutes. Day or night. All she had to do was telephone.

chapter
two

The British attempt on French ships at Mers-el-Kebir provoked howls of outrage throughout France. Frenchmen, who until now saw no reason to distrust the English, had something bitter to swallow at last. The Vichy radio and press lashed out at the aggressor. A BAS LES ANGLAIS! A BAS L'ANGLETERRE! were to be seen scrawled over pavements from Marseilles to Menton.

Letty had not left the house for days; she got her news from the BBC; she went down to the market innocent of what she was running into. She did notice one of those scrawls and at once dismissed it as she would the markings in a public lavatory. Standing in the bread queue, she became aware of a new glacial hostility emanating from the backs of the women. She was not surprised when someone behind her gave her a jab with an elbow and hissed, "Dirty foreigner!"

There was no doubt about Letty's foreignness, nor indeed about her nationality. Head and shoulders above the native Latin women, her pale corn-colored hair and blue eyes were as unmistakable as the Union Jack. She did not have to open her mouth. She did not do so now. She looked down at the woman, a detached look, as indifferent as though an inanimate object had blown against her. The woman subsided.

In the vegetable market Letty realized that the same woman was following her. She had collected some cronies and they all kept a few feet behind her. They did not accost her but made remarks intended to be overheard. Their talk began to attract an audience. Letty felt her arm grasped and turned, startled. "Frank! You shouldn't spring out of the ground."

He propelled her through the women and out of the market square. "You'll have to stay put," he said, "until this blows over." He kept her moving at a good clip straight to his shop. He unlocked the door and locked it again behind them. She followed him on through to the machine shop, one corner of which she noticed had been cleared of tools and old iron. He had pushed the table over there and he had got hold of two easy chairs. She sank into one of them and he poured her a glass of red wine.

"They were like those yapping dogs," she said. "Those wretched creatures that are always chained up."

Frank took his own glass and sat down. "For the time being," he said, "I think I'll do your marketing. They don't notice me."

It was true that Frank spoke French French and—now that Letty looked at him as a stranger might look, objectively—he looked French.

"My French blood will tell. Not highly prized . . . in Canada but, my God, I shall make it pay off here."

Letty sorted out her ration cards and handed them over. She said that Robert in the Bar Bleu kept cigarettes for her. A package a day, or he would sell the whole week's supply on Saturday. That's the most necessary, she said.

Frank prodded his basket which held tomatoes and onions. He said he had a tin of tuna in the house and black olives. There was bread. They could make a sort of salade Niçoise and eat down there. He would take her up the hill during the siesta hour when the streets were quiet.

"I'm ravenous," she said.

At the gate Letty asked Frank if he would come in and help her carry the wireless upstairs to her bedroom. She hated sitting in that large drawing room in the dark and yet she couldn't bring herself to put up blackout curtains for the twenty minutes of news at nine o'clock.

The wireless was a good-sized cabinet one and stood in full view of anyone who walked past the windows. Frank turned to Letty. "Didn't you know," he said, "that you could be arrested for having that?"

She shook her head. She added quite firmly that she could not get along without it.

He lifted one side and found it lighter than he had thought. "Let's go," he said. "At least it's less noticeable upstairs."

Afterwards, when it had been placed on the far side

of Laura's giant, almost square bed so that Letty could reach out and turn the knobs the first thing in the morning or the last thing at night without having to move, they went downstairs. Letty led Frank out to the terrace facing the sea. She wound down the awning and said that this was her living room, the place where she spent most of her time. Frank wandered over to the balustrade. Beyond the rooftops the sea stretched to infinity. Letty spoke, half to herself. "It *looks* so beautiful. As it has always looked. The way it looked last summer and the summer before. That is what I find so hard to understand—that the face of the earth hasn't changed."

"We ought to be damned glad it hasn't," he said. "We've confusion enough to contend with."

She offered him a drink and he refused with a glance at his watch. She was all apology; she had forgotten about the shop.

"That has been long since dead," he said.

"Surely the fishermen still go out? And they will need equipment." Letty said this last as though by saying it she would create business for him.

"They don't go out any longer," he said. "Why should they? They make a fortune selling their petrol ration on the black market. The only petrol to be bought in Free France."

"It's difficult to believe," she said. "Now, when there's nothing to eat."

Frank shrugged. He said they probably rowed out and laid down a net or two; they'd bring in enough for themselves.

Letty said she wasn't thinking of them.

He glared at her. "If you think anyone gives a damn for anything beyond his own nose, you're mistaken."

Letty answered mildly that he had been doing just that; he had been looking after her the entire day.

Letty found that staying at home because she had to was quite different from staying there because she wanted to. For the first time in her life she had an empty feeling which she thought was loneliness. It was definite and acute like hunger. Lonely for whom or for what? She did not want to see anyone particularly. John and Laura, but not in the present circumstances. As it used to be, yes. Perhaps it wasn't loneliness but nostalgia for the past?

She found it difficult to concentrate on the present. She tried to make herself think about it. She enumerated the terrible events which had led to this dead end. Each skidded across the surface of her mind. She could horrify herself by repeating certain facts: that German observers were stationed in Marseilles, that the Roy René hotel at Aix had been taken over by German officers; that the Germans were everywhere they wanted to be, and that they were in complete control. But the horror was of the kind one gets from books, not life.

She looked at her watch and saw that only a few minutes had passed.

She settled herself in a chaise longue on the terrace with a stack of books she'd always meant to read. After a few pages she put the first book down and picked up another. She could follow a sentence or two and then she lost the thread.

Manual work helped most in making time pass: tidying her room, cooking, washing-up. She did these things as slowly as she could. Even so, the large part of the day was ahead of her. For a very short time she became excited by the idea of spring-cleaning the house, room by room. Then it occurred to her that no one would notice and that the first room would be dusty again before she finished.

Frank came every day with her supplies. He let himself in by the back way; it was a shortcut and he didn't want to startle her by ringing the front bell. He never stayed long. He looked gray and tired and said he had to get back to a job of work he was doing. Letty said he looked as though he ought to get out in the fresh air.

"Fresh air? Fresh air!" He gave a hoot of laughter. "I have more than enough of that."

Letty eked out her days by wandering through the back gardens, shears in hand. It was the wrong time of year for pruning, but the clippers gave her a sense of motive. She had just spied out a bush with dead roses when the bell at the front gate rang. She forgot about Frank's warnings and the binoculars he had brought up for her. She rushed into the house for the key. She didn't care who it was, it would be a change.

Through the iron grillwork she saw Juanito—stocky, upright, smiling. He was holding the bridle of a horse. "I've brought some things for John," he said.

John and Juanito had been friends since the Spanish war. Juanito had come to Cannes because that's where John lived, and soon afterwards he started a market garden a few kilometers from the outskirts. Letty thought he would take it hard, the news that John had gone.

She opened the gate and told him.

He seemed pleased that John had got away. "In times like these," he said, "it is best to be in one's own country." He looked up at her with concern in his eyes. "And you, Madame Letty?"

She said that she was guarding the fort, looking after things. She explained that she had had to move into John's house to keep other people out.

"And now we must look after you," he said and nodded for her to open the other half of the gate. Leading the horse and cart, he said that he had come with food for John as soon as he'd heard about the outbreak of feeling against the English. He stopped the cart at the kitchen door. He seemed perfectly familiar with the house; he carried everything straight along to the storeroom where the vegetable bins and crates were. As he emptied a sack of potatoes, Letty said, "So they still exist."

He said he grew potatoes for himself. He stacked the vegetables in the bins and sat back on his heels. His whole business, he said, had been changed by mobilization; his men had had to go. He knew about war, so he planted things to keep his family alive. He took some things into Cannes, but not as he used to.

He stood up and Letty remarked that John had told her once that he was a university professor.

"Biology, an offshoot of gardening," he said, "and not half as satisfying. Growing things can be a great consolation."

Letty said that Laura had put in tomato plants at the time of Dunkirk. He asked to see them. There were a dozen sturdy plants covered with green fruit. "I wonder why she put them here," he said, "when she had that cultivated ground where the cut flowers used to be?"

"She said she was in the mood for hard work."

Juanito walked over to the former flower bed and picked up a clod of earth. He let it fall through his fingers. It was good rich earth, he said.

"I've nothing to plant," said Letty.

He smiled and said not to worry about that. He would bring some plants on Monday if she would have the ground turned over and raked fine. He went with her to the garage and picked out what he thought was the best digging fork.

She waved him off at the gate and locked herself in with a sense of elation.

The next day as soon as Frank saw Letty he asked, "What's happened? Good news?"

"Does it show that much?" she said. "Laugh if you like; I've found something to do." She told him about Juanito and digging the old flower bed and then she showed the stores he had brought. He couldn't keep his eyes off the potatoes. He said he could not understand why they should disappear before other vegetables.

Letty had asked Juanito the same question; apparently the seed potatoes had been eaten or looted. One of the few foods that is also its own seed, he had said, and beans of course. She made a gesture toward them. "Can you stay to lunch or do you have to go straight back?"

"I will stay," he said with an emphasis that made them both laugh.

Back in the kitchen Frank took a package of cigarettes and a chunk of coarse gray bread from his basket. It was all that the day had produced.

On Monday morning Juanito came early, before the heat of the sun, with plants and seed. Letty had the plot ready and he wasted no time. When everything was in he dug small irrigation channels so that the watering could be done without effort. Then they both stood back and contemplated the creation. Juanito said that if Letty would widen the bed by a couple of meters, next Monday he would put in more winter beans. Before leaving he warned her to soak the earth a day or two in advance.

As soon as Juanito was out of the gate Letty marked off the new borders and left the hose running on it. She started to dig the next day. Slow, tough work. She was dead tired by evening and fell into a sound sleep the moment she switched off the nine o'clock news.

It was the first time she hadn't lain awake trying to imagine what London was like at that very minute. She always started out at her own family house. She stood and watched it go up in flames. Then she walked down the center of Ebury Street because buildings on both sides were burning. Her aim was to get as far as Buckingham Palace but something would prevent it, a mountain of rubble blocked her way and wardens pushed her off to Victoria. She never got beyond the doors of the station. Sleep overtook her.

chapter
three

Frank gave Letty the all clear. Cannes had settled back into the old rut; national indignation had split up into the usual daily feuds and bickerings.

Letty did not go down into town at once. She was reluctant to go. She said to Frank that she didn't like to mingle with people who were so wrong, so pigheaded about their beastly ships. Whose war is it? It makes me want to shake them.

When she did go down, it was because she had a sudden longing to be near the harbor and the boats riding there. She paced the quais, absorbing the look of bare masts rising thick into the sky. She thought of Uccello and smiled. Daydreaming along the rue d'Antibes she almost ran into a catastrophe; that is, of finding herself face to face with a Pétainist friend. Just in time she swerved down a side street bang into a young woman. It was a hard bump and Letty grabbed her to keep her from falling. The girl still seemed dazed, so Letty took her firmly by the arm and led her through to the Croisette and to the nearest café terrace, where she made her sit down and sip a brandy. She was a pretty little thing with black poodle ringlets, ivory skin, and velvety eyes, but what touched Letty was the feel of her arm under her hand, small tender bones . . . a child.

"Feeling better?" she asked.

"Oh I'm not hurt," the girl said, looking down at her glass which she turned in her fingers. "The joke is that I've been praying to meet someone English."

"Sorry to materialize so violently," Letty said, and added that she had been trying to avoid an old friend who, she imagined, prayed *not* to meet anyone English.

The girl smiled and looked up at Letty. She spoke quickly once she had started. It was well marshaled and pat as though she had been rehearsing it. She wanted advice, she said, because she was British by passport. Her name was Nina Richard. Her father had been a Tommy in the other war, killed in action. Her mother had married again while she was still a baby, this time a Frenchman. She was brought up as a French child, but her mother had insisted upon her keeping her father's nationality. That had not mattered one way or the other until the Germans broke through in the North. Wild rumors reached Paris about the way the Germans treated the English. Her mother heard that they put them against the wall and shot them. So, she took it into her head to send Nina to the South.

Here she was, cut off. The demarcation line closed off the post as well as people. Her mother could not send money. She couldn't pay her pension bill. The proprietor threatened to throw her out—he wasn't running a charity organization—he'd already confiscated her bicycle. The other day someone told her that the British Consulate would help. What did Letty think, would she qualify?

Letty had been watching Nina and liked her manner and the lack of hysteria. She realized with a pang that this child—was she twenty-two?—this young woman in front of her might well have been her own daughter. "Anyone with a British passport qualifies," Letty said. "I haven't been to Nice yet myself. Why don't we go together?"

"I haven't got the train fare," said Nina. "And what about my back bills? They don't give much, I heard."

"Why don't you come in with me?" The question slipped out, and the instant it had, Letty knew that that was what she wanted. "It's a large house. Come. Come today. It's madness to go on running up bills."

"I can't get away without paying."

"I'll bail you out."

Incredulity crossed Nina's face.

"How much do you need?" Letty asked.

Nina handed her the pension bill.

Letty took in the figure and glanced at her watch. "Back in two ticks," and she was gone.

The bank took longer than Letty had thought. The girl was sitting there waiting, still and white as though struck to salt. The moment she caught sight of Letty, color came back to her face. She said, "I thought the bill had frightened you off."

The girl didn't want to take the bank notes. She asked if Letty wouldn't handle the man, he was so very tricky.

Letty nodded. Of course she would have to be there; she'd forgotten about the luggage.

Nina had two large suitcases which Letty said were no problem because she knew a man who had a push-cart.

If a man were there, too, Nina said, it would be easier about the bicycle. It was a man's, given her by a Swiss journalist who had had to leave. She didn't have a receipt for it and didn't see how she could prove it was hers.

They separated, Letty promising to be at the Pension Rose at 4:30.

Frank was at the shop pottering over his lunch. He wasn't enthusiastic about Letty's having found a stranger to be at the house with her. He objected that she didn't know anything about her or about her opinions. Letty maintained that she was practically a child, and if she had opinions, they were certainly not pro-Vichy. It was self-evident: she was trying to attach herself to the English camp.

Frank swung round the moment he heard the name of the pension. "There's a man who would diddle his own mother. Lead me to him," he said. "I'll fix him."

"We don't want a fight over the bicycle," Letty said.

"I'll get it out of him," said Frank, "if I have to use a can opener on his fingers."

That afternoon when Frank opened the door to Letty, he was dressed in a dark flannel suit, white shirt, and tie. She wouldn't have recognized him in the street. She said as much, which seemed to give him particular satisfaction. He wheeled out the cart and together they walked down the center of the empty street. At one point Frank glanced at his watch. "I'm glad we're early," he said. "He's a heavy drinker and needs his siesta. We may catch him fuddled."

Letty stopped in her tracks, opened her bag and held out the folded bill and bank notes. Frank shoved them into his pocket.

The pension was most depressing: high, ugly, and with scabs of peeled paint. Nina came running down the steps to meet them. She was packed and ready; her cases were in the office. They followed her into a dim corridor at the far end of which Letty caught sight of a wispy maid as she disappeared through a door. "She's gone to call the patron," Nina said.

"What kind of a bicycle is it?" Frank asked.

"A red Majestic, quite new," Nina said in a whisper.

They were silent until a door was opened by a stocky man in a white cotton jersey. He preceded them into his office, retreating to the other side of the desk and dropping into the chair. He had the vacant look of a person not quite returned to this world. Frank stepped up close to the desk, towering above it. They had come, he said, to settle Mademoiselle Richard's bill. They would do so as soon as her bicycle was produced. The seated man threw back his head to look up at Frank. In those opaque eyes nothing stirred. "At once," Frank barked, "or you'll have Maître Paillard to deal with."

The proprietor swung round in his chair, disappeared through a door and came back with the bicycle. He counted the money, receipted the bill, and struck a bell which brought the maid running. They all filed out, Nina first with the bicycle. No one spoke until they were through the gate and into the street. Frank let out his breath in a low whistle. "We didn't have a leg to stand on," he said. "Not without a receipt."

"You mean that Maître Paillard was all hot air?" Letty asked.

He nodded happily. "But scorching hot to him. He caught him once, good and proper, in a swindle."

The mistral was blowing, which made the day sparkle. Nina appeared to be skipping beside the red bicycle. When Letty pushed open the great iron gate, Nina stood stock-still. She had not expected a private park, trees, and grass. "And what a beautiful house," she said. Letty looked, too, as though for the first time and saw how blind she had been to her own good fortune. She slipped round to the back and opened the front entrance, a door she had not used since she had moved in.

The impulse to feed enthusiasm is infectious. Frank and Letty showed off everything: the rooms, the paintings, pointed out the best views. Nina was entranced. They trooped through the house from top to bottom. Told that she might choose any of the bedrooms for her own, Nina asked to go back quietly and look again. Letty said that she and Frank would be out on the terrace.

John had about two hundred bottles of champagne in his cellar and today, before going out to fetch Nina, Letty had put one of them in the Frigidaire. It seemed an occasion. She had not pictured Frank staying on, and now she hesitated to bring it out. "Frank," she said to his back. He was at the balustrade looking out to sea.

"You are right," he said. "She is a nice child."

"Frank, I put a bottle of champagne on ice."

He turned and came toward her. "You're joking!" he said. "How did you get it?"

"It's John's."

"Just what he'd want you to do, drink it up and enjoy it."

"For tomorrow . . ."

"God knows what will happen."

So Letty went off to the kitchen and when she came back Nina was there talking to Frank. She had not been able to resist the blue bedroom overlooking the back gardens. The one that had a fireplace and a bathroom of its own. "I feel guilty," she said to Letty. "Such a magnificent room, but perhaps it's better for it to be lived in?" And turning back to Frank, "I try to cover my greed by saying that it is good to have someone at the back. Mrs. Innes-Gore's room is on the front. Like this, we'll have eyes at the backs of our heads, as it were."

"Letty, to my friends," said Mrs. Innes-Gore. She handed Nina a glass of champagne.

chapter
four

The Winslow grounds were divided, front from back, by a wall which crossed from the house to the long building containing garages and servants' quarters and on beyond that to the boundary wall. It had been put up by John Winslow to defend his privacy. He liked to be able to sit outside under his trees and not be molested by casual callers. Frank tried to peer through the so-called kitchen gate; it was peep-proof. And when he examined it, he found it solidly constructed. He rubbed his hands. "A pretty good blockade," he said. "It would hold men back for a time."

Letty said that anyone might think he was plotting out a line of battle.

"A line of retreat," he said.

"You've still got a thing about that back gate!"

"Dead right," he said. "A big thing." He nodded toward a stone bench. They sat down and he lit their cigarettes. He reminded her that he'd told her he was doing a job of work. He'd been drawn into it by a man called

Macpherson, an ex-army man working as a volunteer in the British section at the American Consulate. That, Frank said, was a cover job for his real work. He was the local head of an outfit which brought escaped English flyers across the line. A lot of prisoners had escaped during the immense muddle in the North. Soldiers were led out through Spain, but pilots were needed back in England at once. Macpherson's outfit brought them to Cannes. Then the British navy picked them up by submarine. Frank's job was to keep the men holed up and sail them out to the rendezvous. He had a felucca in a cove up the coast.

The hitch now, he said, was the new Vichy police. They hung round the harbor day and night, and that put an end to his shop as a hideout. He would have to change to a place where he could get the men in and out at night. He faced Letty. "The set-up here is ideal," he said.

"What do you want me to do?"

"You? Nothing. Turn a blind eye."

Because of the pictures, Letty said she didn't want attention drawn to the place.

Frank laughed and said she had nothing on him there. They did their level best not to attract attention. They'd come the back way in the dead of night and during the day they'd lie doggo in the servants' quarters. "Even you won't know."

"I cannot very well refuse," she said.

"No," he said. "You can't."

Presently he told her not to say anything to Nina until she had seen Macpherson in Nice.

She threw him an indignant look.

"You can't live on air. You and Nina must get your money started. Macpherson will do the registering. I told him Nina's OK, but he wants to see her himself."

"And if he blackballs her?"

"Out she goes."

"It's that serious?"

Nina came toward them carrying glass jars. When Letty hadn't come back, she said, she had looked herself. She'd discovered stacks.

Bottling tomatoes, Letty said to Frank. Imagine knowing how. Such a good idea.

Frank told Nina that he'd been trying to persuade Letty to go to the consulate. It was downright foolish not to collect the money and even worse not to be registered. What if anything should happen? How could the Americans look after their interests without knowing of their existence?

"You win," said Letty. "We'll go tomorrow."

Frank advised them to take the seven o'clock train and come back during the lunch hour. That's what he did and so far he'd always managed to get on. And he said not to give up when they saw the crowd waiting outside the consulate. They were there for visas, an entirely separate section.

They did as Frank said. There was standing room on the seven o'clock. What he hadn't mentioned was that the whole of Nice would be walking to work. No matter which way they turned, the stream of people seemed to be moving against them.

"I keep forgetting it's a city," Letty said between jolts.

"Half Paris is here as well."

Once Letty stepped off into the street and was almost cut down by a bicycle. Nina pulled her back just in time. "I would have gone home now," Letty said when they came in sight of the consulate. The doors were not yet open and pressed against them was a mob like bees swarming. As the doors opened the swarm bent and flowed inside as though pulled by suction. They followed and pushed into the packed anteroom. A voice said, *This way please*. Letty turned and recognized Edwards, the former receptionist at the British Consulate.

"I thought you'd all gone home," she said.

"I live in Nice," Edwards said. "The wife's French. I couldn't get used to sitting about doing nothing, so I came back to work. It's volunteer work now, you know." He left them and was back at once. "Mr. Macpherson will see you," he said to Letty.

Mr. Macpherson was a sandy-colored man: hair, face, clothes. He asked for Letty's passport and filled in a form which he gave her to sign. He had a deep, quiet voice. "Frank told me you have agreed," he said. "We are having a good run of getting men out now. The Germans haven't had time to stop up all the leaks and Vichy is still in a turmoil. A mechanical hitch would be intolerable at this moment. So you see how grateful we are.

"I know you and Frank vouch for Nina Richard, but we cannot afford the proverbial weak link. If I think she is a risk, I'll send for you to witness her money form. In that case, you'll know you have to get her out of the house."

Letty started to speak but Macpherson went on. "We'll look after her financially and she could live in your own small house. There's nothing against your meeting in the daytime."

Before Letty could get a word out, he told her to hand her form to the cashier, first door on the left; and she found herself in the corridor.

The cashier counted out 2,629.95 francs. The franc, she explained, was pegged to the prewar rate of 175.33 per pound. Letty swept the money into her change purse and turned away. What sort of a lie could she tell Nina? What excuse was possible? She found the British waiting room empty and lit a cigarette. She could say she'd been warned that the police were watching the house and she didn't want Nina involved. She'd put it to Frank. He had got her into this mess.

Nina was suddenly in the doorway. "All I had to do," she said, "was show my passport and sign a form."

"He didn't want me to witness the paper?"

"He said he took me on trust."

Letty didn't tell Nina for two days. She was afraid she might connect it with their trip to the consulate and guess that she hadn't been taken on trust as much as all that. She decided not to mention Macpherson's name. Also, she found it rather embarrassing to bring out; the whole thing smacked too much of melodrama for her taste. At breakfast on the second morning, she took the plunge. She sketched in Frank's story as lightly as possible. She made it sound like a minor domestic arrangement. "It won't inconvenience us," she added.

Nina giggled and then apologized. Frank had come up to her room yesterday with strips of black material to be sewn together for blackout curtains. He needed them at once, before nightfall. He had spun out a tale to make one's hair stand on end, escapades in darkness, a cloak-and-dagger affair of life and death. And at the same time he was swearing her to such dreadful secrecy that she hadn't dared ask permission to use the sewing machine.

"I hope you did use it," said Letty.

"Oh I did. I had to," she said.

In exchange for the sewing, Frank brought Nina a length of chain and a padlock and showed her how to wrap it round the wheel of her bicycle so that it couldn't be easily stolen. Now she could take it with her to Cannes. She was still buying tomatoes in quantity and they were heavy to carry; far easier to push the bicycle on that last uphill stretch.

In a very short time Nina had made herself indispensable. She took over the marketing, no longer a simple matter. One had to wait long hours in queues. And when one's turn came round, one had to muster charm and art and ability as well as ration cards and money to extract a semblance of one's dues. Nina had a way with her in handling simple people. Of course, her youth and pretti-ness helped. After the first day, she had taken the cooking out of Letty's hands as well. She said she enjoyed doing it, which was probably true as she was so good at it.

33

Letty was delighted to be rid of these fiddling chores. She threw herself into heavy work about the house and in the garden. She felt the need of hard physical work. She knew she had to exhaust herself beyond the point of thought; nothing could bear thinking about. The world was a black tunnel without a pinpoint of light at the end. The most she could ask was the obliterating sleep of exhaustion.

It was not a good time for an Englishwoman to live through. German planes had abandoned military targets spread over Britain and concentrated on London. Variations of LONDON BURNS and LONDON IN FLAMES were the black daily headlines. Newspapers and wireless alike predicted the imminent collapse of England.

Nina, on the contrary, fought off sleep; she was excited and curious. Frank had said that she and Letty wouldn't even know when he and his men came and went. Nina lay in bed with her ears cocked. She discovered a strange thing: that the vaunted country quiet was made up of sounds, a symphony of small creature noises. She found this out with the abrupt falling of absolute stillness. She crept to the window and peered out. Nothing. She was about to turn away when a shadow moved under her window, then another, and another. Presently the country quiet began full blast and she knew that the men were now all inside.

She was tempted to tell Letty but she remembered the three wise monkeys Letty had said she should emulate. If she talked, Letty would know that she had gone against all three. As long as she kept it to herself, there was no harm done. It's the mouth that counts, she said to herself, entirely satisfied.

Frank spent more time up on the hill. Nina, with reason, supposed that he had to be on hand in case the police should come poking in. To Letty he made jokes about her prescription of fresh air and exercise. He went to work collecting dead olive logs and sawing them up for firewood. The stack grew in one corner of the garage. It was another weight off Letty's shoulders. She had begun to worry about fuel for the winter.

She had begun to worry about a number of things. It seemed strange to be obsessed by firewood and soap when the fate of England was in balance. Strange to worry about next month's money. Of course Frank was right about the money; eventually it would have run out. The busy regular life they were living (when she was away from the wireless) brought a sense of normality, and it was this that held Letty to brass tacks. Although she may have taken Nina in on impulse, she now recognized her as a responsibility.

chapter
five

Letty read about the smashing of Edward VII in *Nice–Matin*. The short paragraph was headed SENSELESS VANDALISM. It stated that two marble statues, the property of the municipality of Cannes, and situated in the casino gardens, had been battered to bits during the night. One was of Edward VII in yachting dress, the other a bust of Lord Brougham. The police suspected a gang of irresponsible youths.

Letty threw the paper on the floor and strode out of the room. Within a few minutes she came back, smoothed out the newspaper, and said to Nina, "It made me see red at first. Now it strikes me as strange: anti-English activity not being officially acclaimed." She read it aloud.

Nina's verdict was that the municipality probably didn't like its property being destroyed. As simple as that. She had never noticed the statues herself. She might go that way through the gardens when she went to market. If there was a crowd standing round, she'd soon know what was up.

"Do," said Letty. "I'd like to know, too."

Shortly after Nina had gone Letty saw Frank go into the garage with an armload of wood. She went out and asked if he knew anything. He had seen it in the paper and he'd walked over to have a look. He didn't get very near. There was a mob of angry Frogs, going at each other hammer and tongs. Extraordinary. Some of them saying quite openly that Cannes would have been nothing without the English.

"I'd like to have heard it."

"Don't you dare budge," Frank said. Before he had left, the rumor had started that the English had done it to make the French fight among themselves.

Letty confessed that she had more or less sent Nina round that way.

"She'll be all right," he said.

Letty picked up her hoe and made for the vegetable garden. By noon she was back in the house anxious about Nina. Frank came in at half-past twelve and offered to go down and look for her. Letty decided that they should wait a bit longer; it could be those endless queues. She poured out two glasses of red wine and after a while they heard the kitchen gate. A moment later Nina rushed in. "Guess what happened?"

One look at her face and Letty said, "You've heard from your mother?"

"Next best. I found someone I thought dead or a prisoner. René Rouvier, the boy who lived above us. We grew up together. If I hadn't gone to the statues, I might have missed him. He's been here ten days. He thought of going on through Spain."

Frank asked where he'd come from and how he'd got here.

"Walked." She looked amused and said that she remembered how he hated walking when he was a little boy. He'd always save his pocket money for bus fares. "He walked here," she said, "from Normandy." He had found himself alone and cut off behind the German lines. So he started walking. He walked all night, every night, but he never caught up with the Germans. Then the armistice came. He walked on, more carefully now. He said he went off his head for a bit; thought he'd been killed and was in purgatory.

"Poor boy," said Letty. "Can we help?"

"He always falls on his feet," said Nina. "A friend loaned him a flat on the Croisette."

"Wouldn't you like to ask him up here for something . . . lunch or dinner?"

She would like him to meet Letty, she said, and see where she lived. She wasn't sure he had really believed her story.

Frank had been pacing about. Now he stood still, scowling down at them. They had been so ideal, he said, just because they had no friends.

The reproach in his voice made Letty laugh.

He ignored her laughter and asked if he could at least have the young man's address. He took the slip of paper Nina held out and disappeared through the door.

"He has forgotten his lunch," said Nina.

Nina bubbled over with stories about the fun they used to have. Letty learned a good deal about René. Among his many other accomplishments he was a genius at fashion designing. He had already made a name for himself in haute couture before the war broke out and he was called up. Nina had a faint hope that he might stay on in Cannes. He said he would if he could find something useful to do. By useful, she supposed he meant something against the Germans. "I believe," she said, "that now that he has had time to think about that nightmare of a walk, each day which passes makes it more difficult to set out deliberately on a similar trek."

Frank was not seen for a couple of days. On the third morning he stepped out of nowhere into Letty's path while she was hoeing. His appearance was so sudden and uncanny that she was badly startled. He said he was sorry but he did not look it. He wanted to prove to himself that he hadn't lost his touch, he said. His confidence had been shaken by Nina's young man.

"What's the verdict?" she asked.

"Tops," he said. "He is going to keep me supplied with food for the men." That was his worst headache: food without cards. "René can, because he's in with the black market."

"Wasn't it rash to talk?"

"Rash not to," he said. He explained that the boy had outfoxed him at every turn. All Frank had wanted was to tail him for a while to find out whom he met and what he did. René apparently spotted him at once, led him a pretty dance, then walked up to him and suggested a drink in his flat. Frank couldn't ask better, so he went. René handed him a large whisky, pushed him down into a low overstuffed chair, and stood over him with the siphon swinging loose in his hand. "Now tell me what you're after," he said.

"I knew I had to give the right answer or have my skull cracked." He said that he was looking for a French recruit; that he needed someone French to get food without ration cards. René splashed soda into his glass and sat down opposite him. They had had a long satisfactory talk.

Nina had already gone to the market; after that, she was to have lunch with René. She came in at four o'clock bursting with the news that René was not going to Spain after all. "I hope that it doesn't sound silly to you," she said, and went on, watching Letty's face. "Since the Germans have had access to the big Paris houses, they are beginning to speak of the German World Mode. That put René in a frenzy. He is determined to produce here the sort of fashions that only our own women can wear. Defiant, audacious things, is what he said. He seems to think it bad for morale for women to be dowdy."

Letty laughed—not in ridicule—amused.

Nina said, "It's true, you know. It is difficult to humiliate a woman if she is well dressed. At least, it is more difficult to know that you have. That is what the Germans want: they want French women to look humiliated, or so René says."

"A novel idea," said Letty. "I think I shall like your young man." Indeed, she knew she liked him for giving out this reason for staying.

"He sent you the message that he will be delighted to come to dinner the day after tomorrow. Is that all right?" Nina asked.

Only once since the collapse of her world had Letty given a thought to what she put on. And that was for Nina's sake, too. She had worn a tussore suit to the Pension Rose. To play hostess to a haute couture dress designer demanded rather more than respectability. In the end, she pulled on a pair of evening slacks, then went into John's dressing room and chose one of his soft silk shirts from Charvet. She hesitated a moment and picked up a silver-gray cashmere cardigan.

"How grand you look," Nina said when she went into the kitchen for the ice. That lightened her mood and it was further improved the moment Nina brought René out on the terrace. She forgot all about his being a dress designer. He was simply himself, small and slender, and very much alive. Her first thought was: he is only a boy. That idea, too, went by the board. He had a man's ease and authority.

Letty made a joke about the locked gate and said that they had all sunk back to the Middle Ages.

"Much further," René answered. "Then, I should have had a horse, not been one."

Nina said, "He pulled Frank's cart up the hill."

René walked over to the balustrade and looked out. "How gentle life seems from the castle on the hill," he said, "at least at this hour." He went on to say how good it was of Letty to have brought Nina here. He didn't settle down with the drink he'd been given but begged to be allowed to go back the way he had come through the house. He had passed pictures he felt he must look at while there was still daylight. He was silent and absorbed in front of each one. Letty, who had gone in with him, left him to it and went back to the terrace. Apparently Nina had gone to the kitchen. Letty replenished her own glass and smoked a cigarette. Then she went back for René. He was standing in the entrance with the front door open. "Clever to have hung the Renoir just there," he said, "where it catches full sunlight."

"I'm afraid that's all," Letty said.

"All?" he repeated, as though waking up, not certain of what he'd heard. "All? A most extraordinary collection. Each one a remarkable example of the painter's best work. I wonder that you dare expose here"—and he named the sum—"for any Tom, Dick, or Harry of Goering's agents to walk off with."

"How do you know so much about prices?" she asked, astonished that the amount he mentioned was, in round figures, the insurance valuation. "It is too late to hide them."

"At least take the Renoir away from the front door."

"They are insured," she said without much conviction.

"What a hope." His tone echoed hers. Presently he went on, "I know you can't get money from England. If you are ever short of cash, I could always sell one of the pictures. Anyone could do that, of course. I mean I would see to it that you got the highest possible price."

"I don't want to sell," she said. The bad moment had come. Bad, because she had said nothing so far to Nina.

From earliest childhood she'd had an aversion, a block, against explaining herself to others. What she did or did not do was her own affair. Bad, because she was enjoying the role of Lady Bountiful, the mistress of such a house. The moment of truthfulness was being forced on her: Frank could let the cat out of the bag any day. "I cannot sell," she said. "They are not mine." She explained that she was looking after them for a friend who had gone to England.

"We will get money from them, nonetheless," René said, his eyes crinkling with suppressed laughter. "Have you a bank account in England?"

"Oh yes," she said.

"And a checkbook?"

"Several. I never used them. The bank transferred money here every month."

"Listen carefully," he said. "This coast is crowded with people waiting to get out. They know that once out, their francs aren't worth putting a match to. They want foreign currency which doesn't exist here. So they are after checks. Naturally they like some sort of proof that the checks will be covered. Proof of affluence. Anyone who is shown into this room will be happy to do business with you." They were standing now in the drawing room. René glanced up at the Picasso above the chimney piece. "You can have all the money you like," he said.

The day before Nina had ridden over to Juanito's for a rabbit. The dinner for René was to be a feast. Letty ate and talked, not fully aware of doing either. *All the money you like.* Her wish had been granted, at last. Not as she'd pictured it as a child. Gold spilling from coffers. Pieces of eight. The fairy godmother, too, came in a strange disguise. Why were children always told not to wish for money? She had never agreed with that; less as she grew older. She had learned the value of money during hard years of making ends meet. Why couldn't it have happened before? On second thought, it *was* in the nick of time. What would she and Nina have done, otherwise? Suddenly she knew how desperately worried she had been because of the lightness she felt now. Light-headed, even, as though she had drunk too much. She felt the same need of caution, not to give herself away.

"You seem preoccupied," she heard Nina say, and that brought her back to earth.

"Daydreaming," she said. "With René as the good magician." She turned to him, "Your proposal is rather on that order. Water in the desert."

"Perhaps we should act soon," he said, "before people begin to seep away. The rate of exchange stands high at the moment because the demand is so great."

Nina looked mystified, so Letty explained about francs for English checks. René added that he would begin at once, tomorrow, to get a line on exact figures and people. If he should happen to run into someone in a hurry, he would telephone. He had stood up and now he smiled down at Nina. "I have already complimented the chef," he said, "but I have forgotten her *pourboire*. May I?"

"A play of words," he said, holding out a small paper parcel: green coffee beans he'd found in Marseilles.

"Can we roast some now?" she asked, her whole face showing her excitement.

"We've got no butter," said Letty.

The two young French ones exchanged a look. René said, "I'll do it dry, if you'll give me an iron pan."

They all agreed that it should be drunk on the terrace in the moonlight. Letty went out to wait for them. Cannes was in darkness under the blackout. She was alone with the heavens and the sea. Presently the scent of coffee mingled with the night.

chapter
six

René telephoned at lunchtime; as he announced, to thank Letty for the evening and dinner. Contrary to his directness of the night before, he spun out the conversation with chitchat. Sandwiched in between, he said, "That book I mentioned last night, have you got it handy?" She suddenly saw daylight when he said that he'd like to bring up a man who was interested. Would five o'clock that afternoon be all right? He dwindled off and hung up.

Her checkbooks were not handy; they were in her desk at her own house. When Nina went upstairs for her siesta, Letty put on a large straw hat and started down the hill. Her English account had not been drawn on since the March quarter. Quite a sum should have accumulated. Being cut off would not affect that; the bank acted as trustee and handled her investments under a power of attorney, even collecting the pension she got as an officer's widow. The bank manager might well be surprised at her writing out a large check; she had never done so before. A great many things were happening now which had never happened before.

She found three pristine checkbooks in the bottom drawer along with a folder of the bank's half-yearly statements. The June 1940 statement had, of course, never come. Therefore she had no record since December 1939. She examined the 1939 statements, December and June, and tried to arrive at an approximation of the money she might have. She had always been wretched with figures. The longer she looked at them, the more of a muddle they made in her head. There was nothing for it but to play it blind and hope for the best.

After all, what was there to worry about? Time and circumstance protected her. It looked as though she'd never be called to account. The way it looked, she'd live and die in Hitler's fortress. It's a wide-open door, she said to herself. It's money for jam. An irresponsible person would take advantage of it; I, at least, can take comfort that time is on my side. How things can change in a day. Yesterday morning I would have been amazed at the suggestion that I could squeeze anything out of a blank future.

The man René brought that afternoon was extremely tall and gave Letty the impression of being in the diplomatic service—something about the discreet fastidiousness of his dress. Unwittingly, she must have expected some sort of racketeer. Her surprised reaction was a radiant smile, to which he responded at once. He was on his way to England. He looked at Letty and said, "This is a very pleasant foretaste." Yes, he knew it well. His life had been divided between London and Paris. *How* he admired the English now! As they went in through the door he said that he was getting out to join de Gaulle. He caught René's look and added, "Not as a fighting man." He stopped short when he saw the pictures and openly admired them.

Letty offered a drink.

"I don't suppose you have tea," he said.

"Alas."

René led them back to the business in hand. The man opened a small black leather briefcase. "Monsieur Rouvier and I have agreed on three hundred pounds at four hundred francs to the pound."

"Much too high," said Letty.

The man looked across at her with an indulgent half smile. He went on placing the franc notes in front of René, who was counting them. "I am perfectly satisfied with the terms this young man and I have come to," he said.

Letty wrote out a check for three hundred pounds and said, "What name shall I put? René mumbled so."

The man laughed. "Just as well," he said. "Do you mind leaving it blank?" He did not sit down again. His train was leaving in two hours. He took Letty's hand. "My only regret, of course, is that we did not meet earlier."

René walked with him to the gate. When he came back, he dropped into a soft chair.

"A small brandy?" Letty said.

"You can't avoid a scolding that way. Business is business; there's no place for sentiment."

"You can't blame me for being shocked at making money on a man who is risking his life."

"Don't forget that he was going to England in any case. By coming here, he's three hundred pounds to the good."

"That's just it," she said. "And if I gave him the *normal* rate, he'd be more than six hundred to the good."

"My dear dear Letty, there *is* no normal rate. There is no rate at all. There is no exchange; it went with the Fall of France. Francs are worthless except to us, the inmates."

"The British Consulate . . ."

". . . pegged the franc to a fiction. They had to take some standard. The Germans print their own francs, as much and as often as they like. That fact alone is enough to discredit a country's currency. Then when you think they've seized our industries and our products, it's a miracle we're not in full inflation. But it will come. It's bound to."

Letty poured out two pale brandy-and-sodas. "I think I follow you," she said, "but it makes me feel quite dizzy."

"A bad inflation wouldn't suit the Germans' books at all. We're more useful in some sort of working order." René continued to think aloud.

At last Letty broke in, "Why should I give my perfectly good pounds for a lot of worthless paper?"

René laughed. "That's the spirit," he said. "I'll make a businesswoman of you yet."

"That hasn't answered my question."

The effect was as though he had reined in galloping

horses. When he looked at her his eyes actually glittered. "Because," he said, "the rations we get won't sustain life. I, for one, am determined to make our days—last days or not—as agreeable as possible."

"But one can't *buy* anything," said Letty.

"Just wait," he said. "The black market in the South is slow."

Letty looked her distaste and René went on, "Supplies earmarked for Germany. So if you are patriotic . . ."

"I've never known a person," she said, "who can so turn things upside down. Black becomes white the minute you start talking."

He nodded toward the stack of bank notes and asked if she had a good place to keep them. She showed him a wall safe behind a picture, which he thought ideal. A professional would spot it at once, he said; fortunately money wasn't incriminating.

"You mean the police?" And then she had to know how they would spot it. René shrugged. The picture was so different from the others, and the only one not properly hung.

"The police aren't picture dealers."

"But they are used to that kind of a wall safe."

chapter
seven

The summer broke with the rains. Water, damp discomfort penetrated walls and was there between sheets at night. Streets were deserted; schools shut.

"What I have never been able to understand," said Letty, "is why it should affect *me* in this devastating way. I was brought up in a wet country; I am used to gray skies. But here in this landscape I could howl."

"It's not like the North," said Nina. "In Paris I scarcely noticed it, an outdoor thing. Here one cannot escape: dampness everywhere, between one's ribs, dripping from one's fingers, mud all over the floor. It corrodes one's very soul."

"The only thing we have is weather," said Letty.

On the fourteenth day the sun came out; the world was back in its proper place, but now with an autumnal chill. Letty and Nina went out of doors to warm themselves. The great double doors, the whole front of the garage, stood open. Frank's rubber boots and then his body appeared down the inner stairs, steep as a ship's ladder.

"Drying the place out," he said.

"No guests?" Letty spoke before she remembered that she wasn't supposed to ask questions.

He didn't seem to mind. "The bad weather," he said.

They wandered over to the sun-trap, a sheltered angle between house and wall where a lemon tree flourished, espaliered against the house. Nina said, "Juanito predicts a hard winter."

"I know," said Frank. "I had been racking my brains on how to heat these digs."

"The fireplace," said Letty.

"And have smoke coming out of the chimney?" he said. "There'd be talk at once. *Why does that English-woman have fires in two houses?*" A solution had come to him quite suddenly; he remembered a stove used in his childhood in the lumber camp. A simple contraption: an iron cylinder with a hinged lid and a drawer at the bottom for ashes. You stuck a straight piece of stovepipe in the center and packed damp sawdust hard around the pipe, filling the stove to the top. When the pipe was pulled out, an air shaft was left where the pipe had been. You lit it from the bottom, and that was that for twenty-four hours. Hot as hot and no smoke.

"Why couldn't you have smoke in Canada?" Nina asked.

"That was incidental," he said. "In that temperature one could not have a fire that went out or that needed feeding since most of the lumbermen were single. Another reason for that sort of stove was that sawdust stood in heaps around the camp."

"What about here?" asked Letty.

"Plenty, now that they've started sawing up small cubes for *gazogène* engines." Frank went on to tell them that he had found an ironmonger in Nice who had agreed to make the stove to his dimensions; that René, when he heard the story, hit the ceiling with excitement. Exactly what France needed. They would make a fortune putting it on the market. He wanted to get things moving. So, early that morning he went to Nice himself in a *gazogène* truck to collect the stove. Frank looked at his watch.

"What will you do when you are rich?" Nina asked.

"Eat," said Frank. "Real food: Meat." That started them off on the meats they liked best: grilled steak, a leg of lamb, or blanquette de veau. But then they both admitted that when the pangs of hunger hit, it was chicken they saw. Roasted, rich brown, with juices beginning to ooze.

"Stop it!" said Letty. Then she added with less edge, "Do talk about something else."

At that moment the bell sounded and Frank went down to open the gate. With a good deal of chugging and puffing a truck came up the drive. René sprang down from his seat next to the driver. His shirt was soaking and he mopped his face. He'd been stoker and forced to sit against the *gazogène* furnace. Meanwhile Frank and the driver were unloading. They carried the iron cylinder and pipes through the kitchen gate and up the broad outside staircase at the back of the garage.

Letty asked Nina what there was for lunch. It had better be good, she said, because her chicken had made her frightfully hungry.

"Chicken?" said René eagerly.

"Talk," said Letty.

"Spaghetti," said Nina, and with a glance at René, "I skimmed off the insects the way you showed me. Tomato sauce."

René nodded. "We'll finish with the driver and come in."

After lunch René and Frank set up the stove and ran the pipe up the fireplace chimney. Frank packed in the dampened sawdust and proudly showed them the cake with the hole in the center. Through the bottom drawer he shoved in a screw of lighted newspaper. He said that it might not catch at once; nevertheless, he placed his hands on either side of the stove. They all stood silent, waiting. Presently he said, "It's getting warmer. Feel."

Nina put her hands where his had been. "It's the heat from your hands," she said, laughing.

He opened the top and peered. He made them all look. Definitely, there was a slight glow. "It will be full blast in half an hour. A watched pot. Come on," he said and ran down the ship's ladder. In the garage he faced them with a happy smile. "Well," he said, "let's celebrate."

"How?" said Letty. "What with?"

Frank looked round at the big useless car, the gardening tools, the sacks of sawdust, at the neat shelves. A box of copper balls stood on one of them. "We'll play boules," he said. "It's as near a ritual as you can get down here."

"I don't know how," said Nina.

"You'll be my partner," said Frank. "I'll show you." He drew a line with his heel and threw the marker. With some solemnity he held out his ball and gave his hand a backward twist—the ball dropped cheek by jowl with the smaller one.

Letty nodded at René. He walked behind the line, aimed, and knocked Frank out to the grass.

"In this case," Frank said to Nina, "get as near the little ball as you can." With beginner's luck and anguish, her ball stopped within a few inches.

Letty played with style and casualness. She sent Nina's ball flying and her own almost touched the marker. Nina groaned. The gate bell clanged. Letty said, "Juanito never comes at the end of the week."

Letty put her balls on the ground and Frank handed them back to her. "We are engaged in the great Southern Game, the best excuse," he said, "for people to gather together."

Letty went off with the key, and Frank hit Letty's ball a resounding crack. "We'll let them hear us play," he said.

"It's a horrid game," said Nina. "Everyone is beastly."

René knocked Frank out, but by this time none of them could keep their eyes from the direction of the gate. Letty was on her way up the drive with an old man and two women. She looked unperturbed.

Frank touched Nina's arm. "Play to be near." She made a not-bad throw.

"Waiting for you," René said to Letty, who had come within speaking distance.

The old man and two women passed with a friendly *Messieurs-dames*. Letty saw them to the kitchen gate and came back, saying, "They pick the olives every year. I'd forgotten they come so early to clean up under the trees." She turned to Frank, "Will it be all right?" nodding toward the garage. "They are counting on the oil and so are we."

"It will have to be. Anything else would be damned silly."

"Shall we finish?" said Nina. "I want to see who is the meanest person here."

"Yes, let's," said Frank. "Obviously, boules is the quick answer to surprise visits. Nobody down here would suspect a game of boules."

At the end Nina said, "I'd like it better if I didn't get so angry at being knocked out all the time."

"Excellent training, my dear," René said with an irritating pat.

An upstairs window was flung open and Frank beamed down at them. They could feel the warmth as soon as their heads came above the garage ceiling. The heat was pleasant and they congregated round the stove. "I wouldn't mind spending the evening here," said Nina. Letty examined the stiff little sitting room with the tables and chairs aligned just so. "You've done nothing to make it comfortable."

Frank snorted. "The whole idea is to keep up an uninhabited look."

There was a brief silence; then the other three gave tongue: *"What about the hot stove?"*

"Damn!" Frank struck his head with his hand. "Damnation," he said.

René pulled an easy chair to the stove and subsided. Presently he looked up. "It must be Letty. And she must be using this room for something she couldn't or didn't want to do in the house."

"Growing mushrooms," said Nina. "People do in Paris."

"Horse manure all over the place? No. Definitely, no."

Frank stood apart, his face to the window.

"Can you paint?" René asked Letty.

"Watercolors when I was a girl."

Frank turned round and said, "Look. If we put up an easel and lay out paints and a few dirty paint rags, the police or Germans or whatever they are aren't going to ask for a demonstration. You," he said to René, "you've been to the Beaux-Arts; you can throw together a half-finished canvas."

"Done," said René. "I'll bring the props."

They did spend the evening round the stove. The warmth held them and René said he wanted to know more about its performance before putting the stove on the market. Frank was eager to show it off. He said he would even cook their supper on the top: onion and tomato soup.

Blackout curtains were fastened tight, chairs were pulled out any which way, and the party ripped. Letty smoked like a chimney, something Frank did not allow his men to do. They had to go down into the garage to smoke. René said, "Now that this is Letty's studio, they can smoke their heads off."

"Not if they have Virginia tobacco, they can't," said Frank.

In a few days René was going to Vichy. He had lined up some rich men there to back his fashion project. He would have to spread his net farther for the stove business. Perhaps some of the same men would do for both. They had pots of idle money. And what was there in the South to invest it in? He would form a company and he (as organizer) and Frank (as inventor) would be allotted shares. He advised Letty to come in on the ground floor. "You will triple, quadruple, your capital in a year," he said.

"How can I?" she asked, lifting empty hands.

"We'll arrange that," he said.

"How do you like the way it heats?" Frank asked.

"Fine," René said. "You'll make a packet."

"Can you see that it happens," said Frank, "before my stomach withers away?"

René laughed. "I'll take note of it. There's no reason why the company shouldn't pay a lump sum down for the invention."

"Not if it cuts me out of the profits."

"As an idealist, I'd say you were pretty greedy."

"Who says I'm an idealist?" Frank sounded aggrieved.

"You're risking your skin for an ideal."

"Rot," said Frank. "There's nothing more down-to-earth than what I'm doing."

"Have it your own way," René said. "You and the moles. Lump sum *and* profits."

"Everyone is going to be rich except me," said Nina.

"A matter for your future husband to solve," René said.

"You will arrange that, too, I suppose?"

"Exactly what I am doing."

Letty sat up. "Do you mean to say?"

"We mean it," said René, "but we don't say it. Yet."

chapter
eight

It seemed that René had been gone forever; in actual time it was just over three weeks. He came back brimming with success. The stove project had caught on like wildfire. Frank had been granted a lump sum as well as a block of shares. The shares were going so fast, he had used Frank's money to get Letty in on the ground floor. Already the company had taken over an abandoned factory and stoves would be on sale by Christmas.

Neither Frank nor Letty looked very pleased. René was taken aback. Why pull long faces when he was pouring money into their laps? "Oh!" he said, shifting mental gears. He would write out a check for Frank the next day—now if he liked—and he had a cast-iron plan for Letty.

Frank's expression changed at once. René put his arm through Letty's and drew her toward the terrace. Scarcely out of earshot she began protesting that she could not write another large check so soon. René made a damping gesture that meant hold your horses. He had taken that into account, he said quietly, and was on a different tack. He would sell a check that wouldn't be cashed for years. There were a number of people, Jews for the most part, who could not—for family or other reasons—leave the country. They had bulk money on them which was an embarrassment, forced as they were to sudden and unobtrusive flight. They had begun to buy English checks because they were easier to carry and easier to hide if they were caught. René smiled and added, "A profitable investment should England win. If England does not, they are sunk in any case."

About his own affairs René said little except that he had the financial backing he needed. Now it was up to him to get busy. He lost no time in doing so. He was everywhere at once. He rented and fitted up a workshop complete with sewing machines and experienced women. He took a suite at the Carlton as a showroom and office. He picked up a couple of stunning mannequins stranded from Paris. He bought a Bentley (probably abandoned on some wharf) for a derisory sum and had the new wood-burning gazogène installed. Being able to cover the country was absolutely essential, he explained to Letty.

Letty held her breath when she saw so many horses put before the cart. The cart being the cold sober fact that material, any sort of cloth, was unbuyable. It was not to be found on the market. It did not exist, a condition not confined to the Riviera, as Letty had learned from people who had scoured Marseilles and Lyons.

"Trust your uncle," said René, and had gone off in the new car. At last he was back and invited Letty and Nina to come and view his treasure.

Walking down to the workshop he admitted that he had made a number of trips, drudging like the single-minded ant, depositing a load and setting out again. When he switched on the lights the room was a dazzle of gold brocaded silks and silk stiff with crimson and silver thread. The women's astonishment changed to a battery of questions. He raised his hands for a cease-fire. Churches and monasteries, he said, if plied with foodstuffs and cash, opened their coffers.

"You are not ashamed?" said Letty.

"He was educated by the Jesuits," said Nina.

René led them over to a stack of handwoven linen. "This natural tone can be dyed any color of the rainbow," he said. "I shall set the ball rolling with a complete collection, day dresses as well."

René was not smug about his success. To be smug one has to rest, for that given moment, upon one's laurels. Up to his neck in work on the opening collection, he began negotiations for future materials. He made contacts for securing raw silk from Italy, an easy matter compared to breaking through the crust of the silk merchants of Lyons. This last he accomplished by the irrefutable argument that it was better to sell to him than to have their stocks seized by German "observers." The Free Zone was dotted by these officers who sent back to the Fatherland any stores of value which they could lay their hands on. And they were obviously well informed.

René did not leave Letty and Nina in peace either. "You shall play an important part in my opening," he said.

"How can we?" asked Letty. She looked down at her work-worn hands and old garden slacks.

"You will see," he said.

A few days later he brought a small satchel of beauty products not one of which Letty and Nina had set eyes on since the armistice. "The Elizabeth Arden man," he said, "is pro-English. He asks nothing better than that his stocks should fall into the right hands."

"He's not giving them away?" asked Letty.

"You might put it like that," he said. "He's letting them go at prewar prices."

This was no comfort to Letty. Never in her life had she been able to afford expensive cosmetics.

"This or nothing," René said, reading her thoughts.

The gritty gray paste now sold as soap had burned Letty's face and neck. A sparing use of olive oil kept the skin from cracking; that was all that could be said for it. Letty succumbed the moment she spotted a box of soap: pink, scented, marble-smooth. Why shouldn't she have something she longed for? If she could buy nebulous stove shares, why not immediate pleasure? She caught sight of Nina's face as she unscrewed a lid and sniffed. Letty gave in.

"Now about your hair," said René.

"Shouldn't all this go down on expenses as overhead?" Letty said blandly, half-joking.

René's eyes opened wide. He spoke in a pained tone. "You owe it," he said, "to yourself as a woman."

Letty was silent. It was a novel conception to suppose that she owed herself anything. She and her self had always been too closely linked in paying off arrears to society.

"You can't let yourself go just because the world has," René urged.

At times René's logic made her feel quite hysterical. This time she didn't have a chance to argue because he had already rounded on Nina for hiding her curls under a scarf.

"Everybody does . . ." Nina began.

"My poor child! A proportion of well-dressed women wrap up their heads and the rest follow. Why?" He paused. "I'll tell you why it started. There was no longer any bleach for the dyed blondes and they had to cover their piebald hair."

Nina looked stricken. "All the more reason for following. I shall go on wearing a scarf. You, too," she said to Letty.

René laughed. "Darlings, time is up. Months have passed. Only the empty fashion remains. The unaccountability of fashion!"

"Not at all," said Nina. "No one can buy a hat."

"I don't want you to wear a hat. I want your black poodle curls shaped to the head. A riot of ringlets. Lovely! There is one simple rule: make the most of yourself."

Letty stifled a yawn. "It's not simple to know what that is," she said. "And isn't it rather beside the point under the circumstances?"

"Very much to the point, the point I'm fighting for. The army has left the field. I'm rallying the women. It will make a difference," he said, "in the end."

Letty allowed her mind to evaporate each time René got on to the patriotic aspect of dress designing; she began to focus again when he switched to the Carlton. A haven, he called it. The last stronghold of the International Set. Outstanding individuals from every country. Enemies, a good many of them. And not a word of war or politics in the public rooms, an atmosphere as smooth as silk. Manners? Self-defense? Whatever it was, it worked. A peacefulness that was startling to anyone coming off the streets.

"A good place for you," he said to Letty. "The next time there's an uproar against the English, you can have my office. Better than being locked in up here."

"What do they talk about if not the war?" she asked.

"The things they talked about before: luck at the Casino, the daily round larded with gossip. An added attraction is the endless discussion on what you can't buy and ways of getting around it. It's a game to them."

"I don't think I should like that," said Letty.

Nina had been stealing glimpses of herself in a dark Venetian glass. "I still can't imagine," she said, "the part you want us to play. Your mannequins haven't gone, have they?"

"Lord no," said René. "I'd like you and Letty to dine with me at the Carlton a few times before the opening. I'll take the measurements now." And he pulled a tape from his pocket. He handed Nina a paper and pencil and motioned Letty to stand up. "This goes on overhead," he said.

"What does?" Letty asked.

"Evening dresses."

"You are going to make the most of us?" asked Nina.

"I am, indeed," he said, sticking out his tongue at her. "I am going to turn their heads with you. Letty can be ravishing. And more important, undoubtedly a lady. And you?"—in a light teasing voice—"A very pretty little thing."

"Are you timing it properly?" said Letty. "Our hairdos will have collapsed."

"We are going to get your hair into good habits. The sooner, the better," he said.

The first time Letty went down to the workshop for a fitting she was struck by the hierarchic atmosphere of René's kingdom. A trim young thing escorted her to the dressing room, a distinguished-looking older woman helped her off with her dress and breathed that Monsieur was expecting her. After a short wait René came in. He examined her neck and shoulders and pivoted her. "Good," he said. "Very good. I was afraid you might be brown to the base of your neck and then white." He slipped off the shoulder straps of her shift and looked at her back. "A décolletage to the waist." He looked pleased and held out a hoop of stiff beige muslin for her to step into.

"Are you going to dye that?" said Letty, disappointment in her voice.

René became himself. He hooted with laughter. "A basic model," he said. "I can't chop around on my precious brocades. What if I'd had to cover you to the chin?

66

As a matter of fact," he said, standing back, "you don't need anything covered. We'll emphasize shoulders, figure, and the smooth brownness. A heavy gold silk, the skirt a long sheath."

At the second fitting Letty fell in love with the dress. She had never touched silk of that quality, and when she walked about it was as though she were wearing her own skin.

"You are a genius," she said to René.

"I know," he answered mechanically, not putting any weight on it. "Would you like to see Nina's dress?" It was a deep red velvet, the color some roses have, with a full skirt. "I had to build up her figure," he said.

She saw at once how well it would suit.

Nina could talk of nothing but the Evening-To-Come. This irritated Letty less after she had demolished her own minor problems. Her evening wrap was shabby and the wrong color. Then she remembered Laura's coat closet. It was packed with coats for every occasion. No matter that she was shorter than Letty. She was stocky, and a cloak could be three-quarter length. Letty felt so virtuous about not taking the mink that the velvet cape with a gold lining which she finally chose gave her no sense of guilt. She had often borrowed an evening bag from Laura. They were all there neatly wrapped in tissue paper. Her own pumps would have to do. Laura's feet were quite a different size.

René was to call for them in the car. Letty said it was nonsense to start up a *gazogène* fire for that distance. "Not if it is to keep my dresses from trailing in the dust," he said. She found no answer to that.

Letty had often gone to the Carlton to dinner and dancing. Suddenly, now, she did not know what to expect. It would be full of strangers. "The last stronghold of the International Set," she grumbled to herself as she led the way through the doors.

She walked bang into Broni. He was an old friend of the Winslows and always to be found where there were beautiful women. He held out both hands to her. "Letty! A vision. I am dreaming."

Mary Fowler was there with her usual entourage. Letty was astonished that she stood up and walked over to greet her. The International Set must be very dull, she thought.

"Darling," said Mary, kissing her cheek. "Just back to the old haunt. Can you believe it? I've been thrown out of Monaco. Imagine, that place!" And turning to Broni, "What a huddle of old friends."

Indeed, Letty thought. The past had risen. In the center of the room sat Dorothy, Isobel, and Charles. Lalla and Eve with some new man.

Broni led them off to his table for apéritifs. As soon as the froth had died down, Letty asked him how he happened to be here, in Cannes.

The face he turned to her was grave. "At the height of the débâcle, I was posted to Ankara. There was no boat. By the time there was one, my papers were not honored. Poland is no longer a country, they said."

"You couldn't fly?" she said.

"No planes."

"Poor Broni."

"Yes," he said. "Poor Broni."

When they escaped to the dining room and Letty was alone with Nina and René, she sighed audibly. "How could you bring me back into all this?" she said to René.

"Just what I need," he said. "To catch them from the inside."

Thin hot buttered toast was brought and René officiated over a dish banked in a snowy napkin. "We must eat this invisibly," he said. "It's something I found myself in Pau." He gave them each a wedge of foie gras marbled with black truffles. For some time no one spoke.

Afterwards, finishing off the champagne, Letty smiled at René and apologized for her outburst. "I was not prepared," she said. "I see now that it isn't at all like the past. Mary would never have got up to say hello and Broni wouldn't have rushed me. I'm a different person; not the poor relation. Partly your dress? It gives confidence. But I think something about the war itself has changed things. Cut people down to size."

"It does that," said René. "And we must watch out that the knife doesn't slip."

chapter
nine

"One cannot go on playing Cinderella; so many of the guests are old friends." Letty brought this out after the second dinner at the Carlton. "They are pestering me, asking me to lunch or to the Casino. I can't very well, in slacks and an old pullover."

"What you wore when I first saw you," said René, "suits you down to the ground."

"Mary asked where I'd got that heavenly gold dress."

"You told her?"

"That was the point, wasn't it?"

"There is another dress for you in the works now; I wanted a new knockout for the opening. One fitting is enough. Tomorrow at lunchtime?"

René worked his imagination hollow for a gala première. The Carlton agreed to loan him a reception room, free of charge, because it was to be an after-dinner *spectacle* which would bring in outside diners. With dancing forbidden and music frowned at, the hotel encouraged anything that might amuse the guests. René also knew how bored everyone usually was after dinner, and how mellow they could be made.

He roped in a Beaux-Arts chum who was a wizard with lighting effects. The one stipulation René made was that the women should be able to see to write down the dresses they liked. Each woman as she came into the room was handed a stiff pad with a pencil attached by a cord. (Bridge score pads with the cardboard back reversed.)

The show had been well rehearsed, each number appeared on cue, and the mannequin on the floor was actress enough to hold the room until the other was ready and smiling. It went off with a swing, ding-dong, cleverly spaced by René with talk to give the waiters time to take reorders. He did not want to give the audience the feeling that he was ramming something down their throats, exactly what was happening in a sense. Or rather, René was giving them the chance to do it for themselves.

In the hullabaloo afterwards there were free drinks, disregarded for the most part in the excitement of comment. René asked the women to sign the writing pads if they considered the dress numbers there an order. A waiter would collect them.

Letty and Nina went up to René's office with him after the party. It would take the driver a good twenty minutes longer to get the heat up in the *gazogène* to take them home. René sat at his desk glancing through the orders. "It's gone like a scythe through a wheat field," he said.

"Disregard mine," said Letty. "I had Mary watching on one side and Isobel on the other."

René took Mary's and Isobel's cards from the pile and compared them to Letty's. "The same number."

"That's what I supposed," she said.

"Not the same ones."

"Naturally not."

René rested his head in his hands. "I *have* got myself out on a limb," he said. "Don't you see? I can't not dress you."

"Your idea," said Letty. She looked at her watch. "Time for us to go. *I could of course stay at home.*"

"Don't you dare!"

"I see that we'll work out a compromise." Each was relieved that he wouldn't have to carry the whole burden.

The rains had started in again the next day. Frank came into the kitchen while Nina and Letty were still sitting over a late coffee. Offered a cup, he said, "What's the use of drinking that stuff?"

"It's hot," said Letty.

He poured himself a glass of wine and sat down. "How did it go?"

Nina went through the evening from beginning to end. "Why didn't you come for the dinner?" she said at last. "There was chicken."

"The dining room is too big. All those waiters and people put me off. I found that out the first go. René and I went out and talked to the chef and he gave me a letter to a man he buys meat from. Food to sink your teeth into, and nobody hangs about watching."

"Could we buy meat there sometimes?" Letty asked.

"I'm sure not," he said. "He deals in wholesale orders. Entire animals. It's not a restaurant, either. I don't eat there every day. Three times a week he gives lunch to two other men. I go then. I don't know who they are or where they come from. We don't talk about ourselves."

"Expensive?" Nina asked.

"More than the Carlton," Frank said, "but you get more. Probably the chef gets his cut, too."

"Poor Frank."

"Don't poor me," he said, looking at Letty rather than at Nina who had spoken. "I've got new high hopes for our investment."

"What's happened?"

"You know how I snoop about the streets, listening to everybody. Part of my job, after all."

"You enjoy it," said Nina.

"The damnedest silly gossip. Neighbors slamming each other. 'I wouldn't trust Louisette so-and-so. Smoke coming out of her chimney *day and night*. Monkey business in *that* house.' Makes my blood boil. Frogs. Can't bear to think that someone else has more than they have."

"Sorry," he said to Nina.

"A human failing, not necessarily confined to the French," said Nina.

"The isolation and boredom," Letty said, "is enough to drive anyone round the bend. Aren't you surprised at the semblance of normality?"

"These peasants don't know they're cut off," Frank said. "They've never stuck their noses beyond Cannes."

"Their livelihood's gone. Fishing and tourists."

"They make up for it, selling odd scraps under the counter."

"I can't cope," Letty said. "You're in a bad mood."

"Who wouldn't be?"

"Yes, who wouldn't be? You prove my argument."

It was a threadbare existence at best. The medical profession had admitted to the press that food rations could support life if the recipient stayed in bed. And as often as not one did not get the full ration. Clothes and shoes were reserved exclusively for pregnant mothers and children. Wine was rationed; cigarettes were rationed (none at all for women). Nothing could be bought freely. France was in a state of mourning; therefore music and dancing were forbidden. What do the populace do? One is allowed to breathe, Letty thought. And not everyone, at that.

It was Letty's decision to ignore Christmas. The others would have celebrated it for her sake in spite of the fact that it had never been made much of in France. "No," Letty decided. "The trappings are Germanic."

New Year's Eve was a different matter. René invited them all to dinner for that. At the last minute Letty backed out. London had suffered one of its worst attacks. "The New Year is dust and ashes," she said. "How can I pretend to welcome it?"

In January, as Juanito had predicted, the winter turned savage. Snow to one's knees and there it stayed. René reported that the hot fountain at Aix was solid ice. Had it ever happened before? No one could remember.

Villas in the South of France are not built to withstand the cold. Letty and Nina hovered over an open fire. René moved into the Carlton, which was heated. Frank stayed near his sawdust stove. Refugees suffered the most, stuck as they were in the odd bare room. The lucky few who lived in a pension or an hotel in a large town like Nice scorched themselves in front of gas fires. Then the municipal works began to go haywire. The gas pressure became erratic; on and off a dozen times a day. It was all that life was worth to lose sight of the flame. *Nice–Matin* carried a special column: DEATH BY DOMESTIC GAS.

"Half are suicides, I'll bet," said Frank.

"Not the French," said Nina. "It's not the French way." Suddenly it hit her what her own fate might have been without Letty. She retracted her statement. "I spoke without thinking. How *can* one know?"

The prolonged cold affected the supply of food, both rations and black-market. It was a lean time. Bread, the rationed bread, the national loaf, was the one stand-by. It never went short. "And no wonder," said René, "they go on adding sawdust." Sawdust is what sprang to mind. Everyone said so with a laugh; it was an accepted joke. One day in the Carlton bar when this joke had gone the rounds, a doctor standing next to René said in all seriousness that it was a fact. He had analyzed the composition: husks, some wheat kernel, rat droppings, *and* sawdust. He had gone into the matter because of innumerable cases of dysentery and a spreading epidemic of boils. Obviously, hunger didn't cause it. It was something people ate. "Now I tell my patients that if they continue to eat bread, I wash my hands of their health."

"And what do *you* eat?" René asked.

"It," he said. "Whatever else?"

René made no more jokes about the bread; nor did he tell the others. None of them, he knew, ate bread if he could help it. Driven by hunger, it was better than nothing. He cursed Dr. Vidal's talkativeness. He could no longer eat a normal breakfast. On the streets he was all too aware of the crisscross sticking plaster on the backs of necks, on cheeks, on arms.

Then Letty's favorite barman and her source of black market cigarettes sickened and died within a few days. A young man in his early twenties, cheerful, on top of the world. Carrying heavy trays one day and the next, gone. She asked the patron what terrible illness could have struck so quickly. He gave a hopeless shrug as though doom and the plague were abroad. "One of those boils," he said, "had burst inside him."

She went straight to René with the story. She thought it might be an old wives' tale; perhaps he had been arrested and no one wanted to say. After a moment's hesitation René came out with Dr. Vidal's findings. It was a relief to talk about it.

"Shouldn't someone say or do something?" Letty said.

"Against the *Government's* bread?" René gave her a pitying look.

When Letty continued to be upset, René tried to comfort her. "None of us eat bread the way the French do. Anyway, it's rather rare to have an internal boil. The others are easily lanced."

"The public corruption," she said. "The callousness on such a scale. And to their own kind."

"This is not the time to generalize, or to argue, or to reason. *Save your own skin*. It is the most anyone can do."

With that aim in mind René followed a story that never got published in any of the papers. America sent a shipload of white flour to Marseilles. a gift to be distributed to pregnant women and young mothers in the Unoccupied Zone. These women would have none of it. They did not understand why they didn't have to pay for it. The fine white powder was too white. Suspicion turned to obstinacy when officials tried to force it on them. The national bread was good enough for everyone else, why should they have to bake their own bread?

Eventually the American flour found its way to the black market; at that moment René pounced. The time-lag between Town Hall and the hands of racketeers was considerable, or so it seemed to René.

It was not quick enough to save Nina from infection. Nothing serious, an external boil high on her thigh. The odd thing was that she kept it to herself. When Letty finally cornered her because she saw that she was limping, Nina said she thought it would burst by itself. Anyway, it was a disgusting thing to have.

René got hold of Dr. Vidal. He lanced it in a matter of minutes. Two days later the leg turned red and was painful to walk on. Letty telephoned Dr. Vidal again. With one brief glance, he said, "Erysipelas." Rampant at the moment. Pétain's prisoners in the fortress were down with it: Blum, Reynaud, Daladier. High fever was usual. The wet compresses should be renewed every few hours and Letty should be careful to wash her hands well afterwards; the disease was contagious.

The patient should be given nothing to eat until her temperature was normal. Champagne was the usual prescription. No water, nothing but champagne. It was light and nourishing. Perhaps Monsieur Rouvier could get some from the Carlton?

"Perhaps he can," said Letty. Not by a flicker of an eyelid did she let on that there was champagne in the house. Distrust, too, was a contagion, and everyone was infected.

"Damn him," said René. "He probably carried the germ, Dr. Know-it-all."

Nursing was a role Letty was used to; she'd spent her married life at it. Now she fell into it automatically. The fever went to 104° and remained there for days. Nina was in another world; sometimes she tried to get dressed and escape.

Frank and René between them took over the running of the house. René did the catering in the easy way: he wrote his order to the chef and sent it down with his breakfast tray. The bills for this he simply stacked on Letty's desk.

As the fever subsided Nina's room became a gathering place. They all, separately or together, spent all the time they could trying to keep her amused. The bottle in the silver bucket, the invalid's exclusive diet, by degrees took the place of the Russian samovar. They all joined in. When one bottle was empty another was brought up.

Dr. Vidal continued to look in and to accept his glass. One wondered if he didn't come to lift his own spirits. Before leaving he would glance at Nina's leg and congratulate her on her speedy recovery.

"What does he mean?" said Nina. "It's been almost five weeks. Time, I think, to break up the party."

Spring was in full force. Nina dressed and pottered about the flower beds in the back. In the evenings when the men were there they played boules.

Letty said, "If we didn't know; if we could take things on the surface, this would be a very happy existence."

"Unglue yourself from the BBC," René said under his breath. Letty heard and didn't hear. She ignored it.

chapter
ten

Letty had the habit of turning on the BBC as soon as she opened her eyes in the morning. It was in this half-suspended state that she heard that Germany had invaded Russia. Her first thought was *this will take them away from England.*

She woke Nina. "Something is happening at last," she said.

Shortly afterwards the two men turned up, in a fever of talk. Frank's idea was that THEY would cut through Russia like butter (remember the Red Army in Finland). THEY'd hold all of Europe; THEY'd have oil. THEY'd be sitting pretty to impose peace terms. America wouldn't come in on the side of the Bolsheviks.

"I'm thinking of France," René kept saying. "This will unleash the most powerful force in the South."

"What's that?" Letty broke in.

"The communists, of course. You may not have realized"—and here he gave her a withering, infuriating, superior glance—"that there's been a witch hunt on for the last two years. Any man known to be a communist can be thrown into jail, just like that. The wily ones are in hiding."

"I don't see that *this* helps their position."

"A line straight from Moscow! They will be more actively anti-German than any of us."

"They'll probably try to take the whole show over," said Frank.

"What I distrust about the communists," Letty said, "is that they have to be *given* a line."

"I am happy for my communist friends," René said. "They have been out of things for too long."

Curious how other people were taking the news, Letty and Nina decided to walk into the town. René suggested that they join him for lunch at the Carlton. "Not," he said, "that you will see anything on the faces there." The two women walked the streets and crisscrossed the market. "Everyone looks worn-out and angry," said Letty.

"It's because you don't come down often. And when you do, you don't look into faces." Presently Nina added, "I get the suppressed excitement. But it comes out of thin air. No one gives himself away."

In contrast, at the Carlton they saw at once that an applecart had been upturned. Prince Andrew of Greece and his suite were in the lounge, apart, silent, with grave faces. The hoi polloi roamed, drink in hand, as though in search of something. "They want someone to tell them this won't shorten their chances of getting out," said

René. Dr. Vidal stopped at their table. He bemoaned the fact that the conflict was spreading. "For humanity's sake," he said when he got no response.

"I wonder what *his* game is?" René said.

Only Mary Fowler and her clique sat at their usual table, with the usual bursts of laughter, and the usual round of drinks.

After lunch Broni waylaid Letty and begged her to take coffee with him. How deflated he has become since yesterday, she thought.

Something which he had never done before, he talked about his past, a rambling monologue about his youth, his home, his lands. He was Austrian by birth; did she or didn't she know that? His family seat was near Lemberg and not far from deep forests alive with game. He talked about the early morning shoots and the vodka they drank to keep warm. From that he jumped to Vienna and his life there as a young cavalry officer. By the rapt look in his eyes Letty gathered that this was a high point in his life. This impression was confirmed when he skipped over the later periods. The War. He fought throughout the 1914-1918 war. In the strange aftermath, money lost its value, and he was obliged to give up his quarters in Vienna. The map of Europe changed shape. Lemberg became Lwów. He found himself Polish. After brooding on his estate for a few years, he went into the diplomatic service to get away and back into the sort of life he was used to. Now, at the new partition of Poland, Lwów was allotted to the Russians.

Broni stopped speaking for a moment; then he leaned forward. "Today or tomorrow it will be German. I shall not ever go back."

Letty could think of nothing but empty phrases. Would anyone have a place to go back to?

"I am not a Jew, you know." This was spoken in the same tone of voice, and yet it rang through her head. It was an idea that had never occurred to her.

"Can you imagine a Jew being a cavalry officer in pre-1914 Austria?" This was a nicety Letty had no knowledge of.

"I'm getting out," he said. "Going to Buenos Aires to stay with Rudi Mendl."

"Can you?" she asked.

"Rudi has sent the affidavits. And an ex-fellow officer in Marseilles will get me out. He's rather high in the Abwehr control."

Letty said how lucky that was. She spoke automatically while her mind coiled round the shock of Broni's being born *The Enemy*. And yet. And yet she could not help feeling sorry for the poor man. Behind his words she caught a whiff of dread. She chattered on in an attempt to keep the talk light.

Broni put a heavy foot in by saying he'd lost his revenues, of course. He'd have to live by selling his gold cigarette cases and what jewels he happened to have with him.

That evening Letty approached Frank on the subject of Broni. "If it were a question of life and death, could you get him out? By the overland route?"

"I'm fighting-forces only," Frank said. "He ought to try the Quakers or the Salvation Army. They are pretty good about Jews."

"No one has said that he is a Jew."

"I don't suppose *he* does," said Frank.

Frank's prophecy that the German armies would cut through Russia seemed to be coming true; they covered vast distances. The swooping pincer technique, however, which had proved so effective against the French army did not have the same result here. Encircled, the Russians melted into the landscape and fought on as guerrillas. They fought until they were dead. The retreating armies left only fire in their wake; they burned all shelter and food stocks. *Scorched earth* sprang into the vocabulary of hope.

Hope was difficult to come by in those days. A burst of it was given to the world when Churchill and Roosevelt met "somewhere in the Atlantic" and made a declaration of their joint war aims. As at a fireworks display, one was transported, and finally left in darkness.

Frank summed it up: "Roosevelt spoke without the people of America back of him. He did not say he'd help. No definite promise to hold on to."

"It's the image to the world," said Letty. "A moral boost."

An image did remain.

Snow fell early that autumn in Russia. The Germans were bogged down at the very gates of Moscow. Leningrad was under siege. The war stood stock-still.

Pétain denounced alcoholism as a reason for the defeat of France and decreed three days of the week to be non-alcoholic. No alcohol could be served in cafés on those days.

"Curious that he should discover that," said Frank, "at the exact moment the Germans are in need of alcohol on the Russian front."

Letty found Broni a bore to be with and yet she went out of her way to spend time with him. He was in a nervous state waiting for the Spanish and Portuguese visas to come through. He was afraid that his exit visa would expire before they came. This often happened, and it meant starting all over again.

She would go down to the Carlton in the late afternoons just after he got back from the Casino, because his head was full of figures then. Not that he had been playing himself; he hadn't the money to risk. He made notes of how the play went and later figured out what would have happened if he had used his system. So he would sit scribbling numbers, adding, subtracting, multiplying. Letty never knew quite what he was doing but he seemed to like her to be there to expound on the outcome. Letty preferred listening to this than to his tirades on her fate if she persisted in remaining in this doomed country. Perhaps she wasn't aware of what was going on? Marseilles was packed with German officers, the Roy René at Aix was turned over to them, they were scattered throughout the South. Observers, indeed! They controlled everything that mattered. They hadn't brought their armies down because Vichy was doing the dirty work for them. At the twitch of an eyebrow, they'd fall like wolves on the rest of France. Look at the pact with Russia.

Early in December the Japanese bombed Pearl Harbor. Four days later Hitler declared war on America. According to Broni, Admiral Leahy had a watching brief at Vichy. An unofficial umpire. The Germans respected certain rights because of him. "If the Americans do clear out," Broni said, "you won't have a corner to turn to; it will be the end. Your house isn't worth it. John's pictures aren't worth it. Nothing is. Get out!"

The Americans in the South of France began scrambling for boats. Broni's visas came through and he set about his machinations with professional skill. Money passed at every strategic point. In a comparatively short time he had a place on a boat from Lisbon and train tickets. He told no one that he was going except Letty and he swore her to secrecy.

It was at this high point in his affairs that Broni astounded Letty. He proposed taking her with him as his wife. It was the only way it could be worked. Like light it came to her that nothing on God's earth could make her abandon her present life. The world—anybody—would be startled at the cap-over-windmill freedom she felt now, an enemy alien and virtual prisoner. Was *money* the explanation? In any case, she wasn't going to leave the source of that.

Broni was leaning forward for an answer.

"Your visas would have run out by the time you got mine. I wouldn't dream of it." She sensed the loosening of tension, relief.

He protested in retreat. "I cannot bear to think of a beautiful woman going to . . . ."

"Waste," said Letty to cover his embarrassed hesitation.

"More final than that," he said.

"What odds do you give me? 10 to 90, 20 to 80?"

"You *are* crazy," he said with the beginning of a smile. He knew now that he was going.

She kept his mind on that, asking about the day and time of his train, the amount of luggage he was taking, how often he would have to change before Lisbon. He became absorbed in discussing his plans. As she rose to go, she promised to have dinner with him on the last night and go with him to the station.

"It will have to be an early dinner. Do you mind? Can you, without saying why?"

"No one questions what I do." She said this with a touch of arrogance that had never shown itself in the past. This brought a gleam to Broni's eyes; he liked women to have temperament. Letty recognized the signs and took a hasty leave.

In the street, she slowed down. There was a lot to think about before she got home. People were unpredictable. It was out of character for Broni to sacrifice his last chance—one could almost say his life, because her visas would take months—to help out a woman he wasn't even in love with. But what she really wanted to take in was the revelation brought on by this offer of escape: the knowledge that she was happier now than she had ever been, in spite of the unnatural isolated existence. Why, when she was hungry most of the time and wretched with worry about England?

It was as though an independent life force had taken over, a stranger inside her was in possession. This stranger took a sensuous delight in Laura's house, she liked to finger the heavy silk curtains, sink her feet into the carpets, stare at the pictures. She exulted in being well dressed, in not having to think twice before dining at the Carlton. Best of all was the companionship: Nina, René, and Frank. The talk of danger didn't bother her a scrap. The reality of it hadn't sunk in. She was helping her side and if she were caught, she'd be "out." Her imagination did not carry her further. She had an atavistic belief in her own invulnerability. She was British, after all. The others were aware of this and took care not to puncture this delusion. Her calmness was a valuable asset; it steadied them all.

And so when she got back that evening to find her three friends waiting and dinner ready, a surprise feast of rabbit, she beamed and said she was beginning to discover how happy she was. Frank did not hawk and spit as he would have done had anyone else said such a thing. Nina kissed her on the cheek and René said that that was the spirit. If the Germans could see her face now, they would go home and cry.

chapter
eleven

Broni got off. Letty was surprised that it had worked. Broni, also, to judge from the way he watched the gate leading onto the station platform. And yet, why shouldn't it? His papers were in order, he had his visas, his tickets. That counted, but it wasn't the last word. They both knew that anyone could be plucked away, even from the inside of a snug first-class sleeper. Not until Letty got a post card with a Spanish stamp did she fully relax. Broni was now in another world. She thought of Tom's death and her thankfulness at his release. Absurd to be reminded of that and yet Broni's transition seemed equally final, unthinkable, mysterious.

Broni was the last of the Winslow connections for whom she had felt a social obligation. With him gone, the decks were cleared. Socially, she was responsible to no one (who could be to Mary Fowler?); she didn't have to produce a gracious smile when she didn't feel it; she could be herself entirely. Never again would she allow herself to become enlaced in the social strait jacket. How to manage that in a normal existence, she didn't bother to think; that condition was as remote as Judgment Day.

The war was going badly for England. In the Far East the Japanese had control of the seas and were sweeping the British out: Hong Kong, the Malay Straits, Singapore. In the desert Rommel, who was in full retreat, turned at the frontier of Tripolitania and with inferior forces mounted a surprise offensive of his own. He drove the British back to Tobruk. To Letty it seemed as though some essential tension had snapped in the British fighting man. Frank was more optimistic. "It takes a while," he said, "to get our second wind."

It was after dinner at Letty's house, and Frank, instead of slipping away or challenging Nina to a game of dominoes, paced the floor. It was the sign that he had something on his mind to unload. The others waited, not even finishing their conversation. At last, he spoke. "Vichy is cooking up what they are pleased to call a security measure. My man at the police doesn't know the reason, and he is high enough to be told, if anyone is. All the English, including women, are to be removed from coastal départements to designated villages in the interior."

He thrust his hands thumb-deep into his jacket pockets and glared at Letty. "I've got French papers for Nina but what in the devil can I do with an accent like yours?"

Letty stared back at Frank. "Nina could run the house," she said.

"You are more convincing. Besides, I don't think you could survive without the oil and vegetables from this place. You haven't the knack for it."

"Or the money," said René just loud enough for her to hear.

She gave him a quick glance. "I see," she said and paused, apparently going over the position with an inner eye. "I do know a way out, but I never thought I'd stoop to it." She felt in her handbag and handed Frank her carte d'identité.

He gave a sharp whistle. "Irlandaise. Born in Belfast. And what is this S.B. after Irlandaise? It's written in different ink."

"*Sujet Britannique*. I put that in," said Letty. "The last time I renewed my card, it came back like that, plain Irish. I suppose they thought they were doing me a favor."

"Jacques must have done it. He's probably cleaned up your dossier, too. What a fool I was not to have talked to him about you." He put the card in his wallet. "I'm not looking forward," he said, "to explaining away your tampering."

"Make me angry and I'll refuse. Don't you see that they've been tampering with me? My convictions and loyalty . . ."

"What about Mary Fowler?" asked Nina. She had never liked her.

" . . . Without a by-your-leave," said Letty.

"No luck," said René. "She isn't going."

"Turning Irish, too?" Letty said.

"She's under Ciano's wing."

"Exactly," said Nina with conspicuous emphasis.

"Her sister married into a rather grand Italian family," René said.

"Only a black-hearted traitor would accept it," said Letty.

"I would," said René. "If Ciano offered me a wing —and Hitler—and Churchill, I'd accept them all with joy."

"Are you serious?" Letty asked.

"I'm fed up with martyrs. Two friends of mine were arrested yesterday, young men. They could have got off if they hadn't admitted they were communists."

"Then, why aren't you a collaborator?" Letty said.

René wrinkled his nose at that word with a bad smell. "I didn't say I wouldn't work for my beliefs."

"That is the road to martyrdom."

"I'm not going to get caught."

"For goodness' sake, touch wood," said Letty.

"And you, Frank?" asked Nina.

"François," he said. "Gilt-edged French since the armistice. It seemed the simplest way out. A few English friends wanted to transfer their boats to a French owner. I didn't trust anyone else."

"Phony French papers stand up that long? Don't they check back? Place of birth, parents, etc.?"

"You thought I was pushing you into a hit-and-run existence?"

"I don't see how you make it stick," she said.

Frank enjoyed explaining things to Nina; he settled down to it. "There are several places in the North where the Town Hall has been destroyed by bombs, all records included. You and I," he went on, "were born in Colmar. I chose the largest town because it is more anonymous."

"Shouldn't I read up about it?"

"Your parents moved to Paris when you were a baby."

"They couldn't have done that till 1919."

"You'd still be too young to remember," said Frank. "I'm the one with the worry. I slipped up. It came to me not long ago in the middle of the night. *I was German during the last war and of military age.*"

René said, "Vichy won't poke her nose into the Alsatian muddle."

Frank nodded. "I'm not thinking of Vichy. They have no reason to move the English from the coast. The Nazis are on to something. Spain? North Africa? It means they'll move in."

"We're in the Italian sphere of interest," said René. "Mary says Hitler is giving them the Alpes Maritimes."

"Nothing Mary Fowler says will keep Hitler from doing as he pleases." Frank turned toward Letty and Nina who were murmuring together on the sofa. "A last point," he said. "From now on you should not be seen at the consulate. No more monthly allowances."

"They know all about us there," said Letty. "And what will our friends say?"

"Your friends won't be here," Frank said. "Nor will the Americans if the Germans come down. I'll have Macpherson snatch out your files at once."

Groups of Englishwomen began to appear in the streets of Cannes. There was no mistaking them; it was their clothes and the way they walked. Letty had forgotten how different they were. She lingered in front of shop windows or slowed her steps to overhear what was being said. Apparently they had come from villages all over the Alpes Maritimes and were in a state of excitement to be on the verge of travel and to be in Cannes. They had not been allowed to budge since the armistice. Most of them were staying on a few days. They radiated a jaunty holiday spirit.

Letty was lunching with René and Nina at the Carlton. Not far from them in the dining room was a large round table in festive dress, vases of carnations, place cards.

"It can't be a first communion on a weekday," said René. "Must be a wedding."

The staff liked René and served him quickly. Soon they were eating and Letty started telling her morning adventures when a sharp kick silenced her. She glanced up and across to where René was looking. The large round table was bristling with animation, all middle-aged women with weatherbeaten faces and exotic head scarves. René returned a wave of recognition. "The English contingent from Haute Cagnes," he said. "Forgive me?" He shook hands with a number of them and spoke for some long minutes to the woman who had greeted him.

He came back to his own table laughing. "A last blowout," he said. "They're all off to a place in the Vaucluse called l'Isle-sur-la-Sorgue because the Michelin says it is built along a trout stream. The two hotels list *Truite au bleu* as a specialty. They think the war wouldn't affect trout."

"Does it?" said Nina. "I haven't tasted fish for a long time."

There seemed no hard and fast plan for the evacuation of the English. Apparently it depended on the politics of the village or community. For more than a month Letty kept running into the solitary Englishwoman who had just got her marching orders. These last were mostly women she had met at one time or another, women who owned large estates within a score of miles from Cannes. Letty dreaded these encounters. They obliged her to discuss matters which she felt, by rights, should be hers: how to safeguard house and possessions, maintain vineyards and olive grove, clip hedges, keep the place up. A good many of the women came to Cannes to arrange a fictitious sale to some French friend. Letty could not bring herself to admit that she had slunk out of all of that. If they asked where she was going, she said, "The Vaucluse, it's nearest." If pressed about *when,* she was vague. She was winding up business with her lawyer.

"I hate telling lies," she said to René. "I'd much rather stay at home."

He wouldn't let her. "Remember," he said, "if you run into an Englishwoman in Cannes, you have as much right as she has to be here."

"Mary Fowler is a different kettle of fish," she said.

"Quite," he said. "I don't think she's such an ass as to bring up the question."

"She drinks a lot."

"*And* has influence," said René. "Better keep on the good side of her."

"She hasn't got a good side," Letty said.

.　　　　　.　　　　　.

Letty no longer reckoned time by the calendar but by war disasters. It was after the Dieppe landing that, practically overnight, the Carlton was again booked to capacity. The newcomers were men in their early twenties or younger. If there had been less of them Letty would have sworn they belonged to the same family. "There is a definite resemblance," she said to René.

He nodded; he was absorbed in watching Mary Fowler approach a group of them. Young men were at a premium and these were particularly presentable: handsome and well-dressed. Well-mannered, too, apparently. They stood and received her graciously.

Mary went back to her own table almost at once.

"Fun and games after dinner?" René said aloud.

The young men kept to their own corner after dinner. In fact, they were never seen to mingle with other people; they kept strictly to themselves.

They spent their days on the beach. That's how René saw so much of them. He reported back to Letty, "They are crazy, those kids. Crazy and foolhardy." They all wore a gold Star of David on a gold chain round their necks.

Once when René caught one of them sitting alone on the sand, he went over and started a conversation. "Don't you know," he finally brought up, "that you could be shot for a gesture like that?" nodding at his chest.

The boy looked up and René saw in his eyes that he knew everything there was to know about these things. "Our parents," he said, "if we still *have* parents, are obliged to wear it. Why shouldn't we?"

From time to time René had other talks with the

same boy. He didn't swim out far like the others. In spite of René's prodding and offers of help, he avoided any talk of the future. He was perfectly willing to chatter about the wonderful life here by the edge of the sea, even though it was quite plain that his thoughts were elsewhere. Tackled with it, he said that he hated leaving his mother and father who were in danger and not young. "They forced us to leave," he burst forth, "all of us. There's another witch hunt going on, and apart from that, a new law of compulsory service for work in German factories. One or the other was bound to get us."

"You are not safe here," said René, and from the way his statement hung in the air, he knew that it was old hat.

"I'm going in again," the boy said and walked down into the sea.

That was the first René heard of the STO, *Service du travail obligatoire*. He wrote off at once to his Vichy backers for affidavits that he was indispensable to French affairs in Cannes. In talking to Frank he said, "Laval put this over on us. He says that one POW will be released for each three men who go. Only a fool would trust that German bargain. What it will do is to drive every able-bodied man underground."

"Not if they feed them and pay good wages," said Frank.

Both were right, but neither knew until after the war. Six hundred thousand men had gone into the STO. No prisoners were repatriated. At the time, Frank and René were conscious only of the swelling maquis. The men had to be fed somehow. By leaving home they had lost their ration cards. René did what he could, but it was a very small drop in the bucket. It was inevitable that the maquis would have to live off the land. They formed raiding parties. They broke into town halls and stole ration cards; they robbed large concentrations of food stocks, tobacco shops, banks, and post offices.

In the meantime, René worried about the young men. What were they waiting for? Had their arrangements fallen through? And yet they appeared neither agitated nor despondent. Surely they were too intelligent to stay on like sitting ducks? René made inquiries among his contacts and not one of them had been approached.

One morning they were gone, all of them. Where to? René was intrigued. They had checked out of the hotel the night before. He got this out of the hotel porter and the fact that two cars had called for them. Not taxis, private cars. At the station the porters he knew there assured him that no young men had taken a train in either direction.

Where would they drive in the middle of the night? Where would he go if he wanted to lose himself? Marseilles, but then he knew it pretty well. At the newsstand he bought a Marseilles paper on a hunch and studied the shipping news. That very day a boat was leaving for North Africa. His curiosity was racing: could they get away with a thing like that? North African boats were owned and run by bigoted collaborators. In many ways it was sounder to sail close to the wind, just as he knew that in the North illegal landings were made under the shadow of a blockhouse. No one expected it.

He could not get to Marseilles in time, but if he went today, he might learn something. He had business there in any case. He telephoned Letty that he was going for the night and caught the train. Thanks to his Vichy connections he had a permanent travel permit. Without one, no one could get out of the station at Marseilles.

He walked down to the old port, where he had a bowl of rice and meat in an Indo-Chinese hole-in-the-wall restaurant, one of the few places which still served proper food and which was, in consequence, frequented by men who knew what was what. René saw the man he was looking for, an import-export man who traded with North Africa. They had had dealings before, and so when there was a space next to him at the long table, René moved there with his carafe of wine. After the usual banter, René said that he wanted to find out something about passengers who had sailed on the noontime boat. The man said his manager had been on the dock all morning and he'd be at the warehouse that afternoon. He scribbled down the address and signed the paper so that René could get in.

It was a freighter, the manager said. Very few passengers. No, no group of young men. Some elderly couples.

"I'm thinking of eight young people," said René.

"There were some young Arabs." Two men and four strapping, handsome women. Well turned out, European fashion.

"How did you know they were Arabs?" René asked.

The man thought. "They had the look. I'm used to

Arabs, you know. Then the maid was covered in veils to the eyes. And the manservant who'd been looking after the luggage wore a tarboosh. No mistaking them."

René thanked the manager and took his leave. The old taxi had waited after all, an old rattletrap affair belching smoke from its *gazogène* furnace. He leaned back against the grimy leather. Eight, he thought. Eight counting the servants. Smart to break up the sexes and class. They must have had someone good to get passports and tickets and the right sort of clothes. But then, they had money, plenty of money. And brains. But *was* it the boys? He liked to think it was.

chapter
twelve

Letty was up early that morning. She was out under the trees talking to the pickers about where to store the olives for the mill when she happened to glance at her watch. Time for the BBC. This hour was both habit and superstition, like touching wood. She would clear out the shed later, she told them, and was off.

The instant the wireless was warm enough to speak, the news came through that the Americans had landed in North Africa in invasion force. The rest of the news she heard with half an ear. She found her diary and put a light cross against the date, November 8. Staring down at the page, she was startled to see on the eleventh, printed in bold type, that ghostly reminder: *Fête de la Victoire*.

The Germans also remembered this date. On November 11 they occupied the whole of France.

A sunset curfew was declared. René was away on business. Frank came up to the house to be with the women. The gates were double-locked, the blackout curtains securely fastened, and in the drawing room a cheer-ful fire blazed.

"I'm glad," Nina said, "that we are now the same as the rest of France."

"But we're not," said Frank. "Nice and Cannes get the Italians. The officers look pretty cocky but the soldiers walk about bunched together like sheep." He advised the girls to keep to the house for a day or two. The French resented being occupied by Italians, whom they looked down on as cowards and boobies. There had been hissing and jeering in the streets.

René was in Aix-en-Provence, and there it was the German army that moved in. A number of students had ganged together in a vociferous promenade down the cours Mirabeau. They were quick-marched to jail. At midnight they were taken out and made to walk the deserted streets with their arms high above their heads. René spoke to a boy who had been in on it, and he said that when some of the boys fainted, they were all taken back to jail and released at dawn. It was a soft punish-ment when you think what the Germans might have done. It would seem that they had been ordered to be friendly and polite.

René had had to spend a good deal of time at the café of the Deux Garçons and there he saw that the Germans offered cigarettes to the students. Several times he heard them protesting that they were not German but Austrian. The students remained cool and unreceptive. They refused the cigarettes and turned away from conversation. René predicted that the overlords would soon change their tactics.

It occurred to Letty that Frank's work would be wrecked by the occupation. "You won't be able to spring your submarine trick."

He gave a sharp snort. For months now, he said, all submarines had been commandeered by a higher authority—probably in connection with this African landing. He had cursed the "higher authority," but now he was glad because he had had time to establish safe stops on an overland route before total occupation.

The Italians in Cannes didn't worry him; it was the Germans between here and Spain and the German guards on the frontier. "I don't want any hitches; so I've got down some experts from the North who are used to German habits as guides over the tricky stretches."

What had happened to the French fleet?

More than seventy warships were at anchor in Toulon harbor, the one great prize, the one trump card held by Vichy France. Fourteen days had now passed since the total occupation of France. Not a word about the fleet had been heard from any wireless station; not even Lord Haw Haw had mentioned it.

On the morning of the twenty-seventh a great black curtain stretched across the western sky. Simultaneously the BBC announced that the French fleet had scuttled itself in Toulon harbor.

Letty was beside herself. "*Why didn't they put to sea?*"

"The French and English navies are like cat and dog," Frank said. "Always have been."

"They may not have had enough fuel," René said.

" 'Many captains went down with their ships.' Surely they could be rescued in a harbor?" Nina looked toward Frank for an answer.

"It isn't easy to sink a ship," he said. "Someone has to blow it up."

"They could have used time bombs or long fuses, anything." But Frank was no longer there. He had opened the French windows and was standing on the terrace looking toward the black sky.

"What I long to know," said René, "is what took place during these last sixteen days. What were they doing, the Germans and the French navy? Holding talks? Trying to strike a bargain that didn't work? How did they outwit the Germans?"

"The French stayed just out of reach on the water," Nina said.

"Don't be silly. The Germans had tanks and they'd taken over the defense guns."

In the end Letty agreed that the French navy had behaved impeccably. "Given their limited outlook," she added. The black smudge hung in the sky for almost a week. Those ships would never be used against England.

"What is going to happen now?" Letty asked in the middle of writing out a check. She and René were alone in his office at the Carlton.

"Business as usual," and he gave a half smile. "The Germans will never destroy the Jewish Syndicate; it's too widespread."

"But they are arresting all the Jews."

"They are looking for them," he said. "Quite another matter."

The Germans had lost no time in opening a campaign for the hunting down of the Jews. Unused to military overseers and to that sort of goings-on, the people of the South, already indignant, were further outraged. Almost to a man, collaborator or not, everyone who could took a hand to thwart the Germans. Businessmen's clubs (René had not heard of them before and thought they were American in origin)—the Rotary Club, the Lions Club—sent out instructions for members to warn, and if possible to protect, any Jew in danger.

René now told Letty how a doctor in Aix, who in the early days was often seen at the Roy René with German officer "observers" and who had been denounced on the BBC as a collaborator, had come to him for advice about a Jewish couple he was hiding in his house.

"But why?"

"He's a bigwig in the Rotary Club."

"Why did he come to you?" Letty said in some alarm.

"A fellow Rotarian gave my name. I was bowled over that a backslapping get-together club could do that: turn a political fanatic back to front and make a normally discreet man lose his head. I still don't understand it."

The Italians showed no zeal in the Jewish witch hunt. They were entirely preoccupied in upholding their status. That was easier in daylight. After dark and after the ten o'clock curfew was the dreaded time. They did not patrol the streets by twos as the Germans did. A gang of them would stick together down the open middle of the widest streets. It was convenient for everybody: civilians who were out after ten knew how to get home undisturbed, and there were no casualties among the Italian soldiery.

Jews came to Cannes for a breathing spell; not to the large hotels as before, but harbored by a willing populace. René always had his flat filled, and he persuaded Letty to loan him her own little house for the occasional overflow. Everyone was aware that Germans were in the background; that the Italians were not trusted, and were not likely to last long. Why did the Germans tolerate the situation? Hitler's sop to Mussolini? German manpower was stretched to its utmost limit; let the Italians do something?

Letty handed the check to René and he held out the francs. It was the first time he had done it like that. "I'm an agent now," he said. "They've taken on goyim for field work."

"The exchange is awful. Why didn't we wait?"

"It will not go up," he said. "The demand keeps it down. With prices high as kites, none of the English can live on the allowance. They all come for francs, and if they don't have checkbooks, they write out IOU's."

"Isn't that rather risky?"

He looked at her with flat eyes. "Even if the Syndicate loses on half their clients, they'll make a good 100 per cent."

"I meant for the poor English," she said. It was a tender subject and she was sorry that it had come up. She shoved the francs into her bag and walked over to the window. Someday she would have to talk about her own problems, but not now. That's what she'd been saying to herself all along, *not now*. Why face it, when anything might happen?

"How do the English get their allowance since the Americans have gone?" she asked.

"The Swiss."

"I'm almost glad I'm Irish."

"That's better," he said, moving over to her at the window. "It's taboo to be down-in-the-mouth. If you haven't enough francs, write another check. I'll take you in to see the new dresses. Then we'll order something special for lunch. Why don't you put on one of the new models? I long to see Mary's Italians twisting in their chairs to get a better look at you."

On the day before Christmas the assassination of Darlan put an end to the fiasco in North Africa. The choice of that Vichyite had been so painful that none of them could bring himself to speak of it. Early in the New Year the German army with Field Marshal Paulus surrendered at Stalingrad. The great Russian offensive continued to roll forward. In North Africa the Axis forces were cornered in Tunisia. English and American bombers were making free of the skies to strike at German cities. It would seem that the tide had turned.

"Don't expect too much, too soon," René warned them.

"I heard a Marius story today," said Frank. They looked at him with resignation. "A German officer stopped Marius and asked how to get to the Hotel Splendide. Marius told him and was about to walk on when the officer pointed to the ground and said, 'Where's my suitcase?' The officer cursed the French and cursed Marseilles. 'That's nothing,' said Marius. 'A friend of mine was in Berlin the other day. He did exactly what you did. Put his case down and asked the way to the Zoo Station. A German pointed across the street. The station had gone.' "

"You made it up," said Nina.

"Do you know the one about Marius bombing Berlin?"

"Not more than one a day," said René.

"He had to turn back with his bombs because the all clear was sounding."

"That's funnier," said Nina.

"It was shorter," René said.

chapter
thirteen

Letty heard from Bunny Sutton, the one English friend who knew she was still at Cannes, and René from a number of check-clients, that every English man and woman under 65, throughout the South, had been summoned to report at Cavaillon or at Pau—whichever was nearer—within a week's time "with the object of redistribution."

Bunny's letter was a burst of anger. How *can* they do this? They expelled us from the coast on the promise that we'd be taken to a safe place where we would be left in peace. The notices we got said to bring warm clothes, blankets, and especially money and jewels. It's the sort of order given to the Jews when they are to be shipped off to a concentration camp. Do you think there's been a muddle? Rather worrying. I may try to skip.

"My letters," René said, "are straightforward requests for cash. My men are taking that notice literally. I'll have to go of course, but thank God my lot are all in Cavaillon."

Frank went to his policeman to find out what was

up. Jacques had no information. The affair did not concern the Alpes Maritimes as the English had already been evacuated. He did, however, put through a call to a colleague in Cavaillon and was told that two thousand English men and five hundred women were involved. The whole caboodle was being run by Vichy as a surprise gift to the Germans. Where they were to be taken, no one knew.

"It's against international law to take prisoners from Free France to an enemy country," said Letty.

René snorted. "And what about the Jews?"

"Do the Zones still exist?" asked Nina.

Letty said, "The German army announced that they were moving into the Free Zone to protect it."

Frank hawked and spat into the fireplace.

While René was in Cavaillon, Frank tackled Letty.

"Whether you like it or not," he said, "one of Macpherson's men is trying to get you an Irish passport from the minister in Vichy."

Letty burst into what Frank took for hysterical laughter. He wondered whether he should slap her, but when she spoke it was in her normal voice. "He'll get it all right. The minister is an old friend of John's and mine. It was his perennial joke that Ireland claimed every soul born on the island; that one day I would succumb. He's often promised to send a passport in a shagreen case."

"Are you feeling all right?" Frank asked.

"How do you expect me to feel when I ought to be on my way to prison with my friends and compatriots?"

Frank nodded at Nina to take over, and left them.

René brought back the barest crumbs of news. He had sat in on the mass meeting convened by the Swiss consul. The consul walked into the hall ten minutes late and announced that he was not there to answer questions; in fact, he would refuse to do so. It was his business to pay out their monthly money. His assistant would call out names in alphabetical order. Anyone who did not come forward at once would forfeit his money. Before starting, he said, he would like to reassure them. They would be far better off where they were going than where they were now.

Where's that? Where? resounded from all sides, but the assistant was already calling names.

"As though he were dispatching them to heaven," said Letty.

"Exactly what they all felt," René said, and continued that everyone had been taken off the next morning by a fleet of buses. He had managed to find out which woman was her friend Bunny Sutton. She went off with the others like a lamb. There had been one hysterical woman from Mauritius who clung onto the vertical bars at the end of the bus and when two policeman tried to push her inside, spread-eagled herself across the door. The chief of police came over and threatened her with a punishment camp if she didn't go. She flung herself to the ground and rolled in the dust. Eventually she was led off by four policemen.

René followed the convoy, which drove to the station at Avignon. He was forced to park some distance away and walked back onto the platform. He didn't stay long because there were only the prisoners milling about and a number of German officers watching. The train was immensely long and in each compartment, sitting next to the window facing the engine, was a stony-faced police officer. None of the station officials could tell him anything about the train or where it was going.

Letty's Irish passport came through within a few days and with it the courier brought a letter from the minister. Frank took them to René's office and said to give them to Letty. "I've got a lot of work on these days," he explained.

"This morning," René said, "I saw you sunning yourself for an hour in front of your shop."

"That is part of my work," said Frank and made for the door.

René took the bull by the horns. That evening he walked out onto the terrace where Letty was waiting with the drink tray and handed over the documents. She examined the passport with curiosity and said that it might as well be written in Turkish. The language was strange enough to confuse anybody. She rather liked the photograph.

"We had a snapshot blown up," he said.

She glanced through the letter and passed it over. "He is being very kind," she said. "Welcomes me into the fold in a sweet way, without rubbing it in."

"It is a relief to us," he said. "An Irish passport is the devil to get hold of illegally."

"I can't say it is a relief to me," she said. "Makes me feel all the more guilty. How can I face the world afterwards?"

"You've got the picture upside down," he said. "*We*

did this to you because you are doing useful work for His Majesty's Government. Every agent sent over here has one or more false passports. Don't give it a second thought."

"I still feel a cheat."

"Would it help you to know that if you are caught, you are in far greater danger than those compatriots of yours?"

"Yes," said Letty. "It does." She did not look entirely happy but she stopped talking about it. She gave up her British passport without protest when René said that Frank had asked for it.

Overnight, with no ripple of warning, the Italians vanished from Cannes and German troops were in their place. No question now of dodging home after curfew. These new troops meant business and were trigger-happy. If a leaf stirred at night, they gave it a burst of shot. They shot at any splinter of light which showed in the blackout, and they went on shooting until they got the light bulb.

This threw the happy-go-lucky meridionals into a state of terror. During the Phony War, when it had been possible to buy material, nobody had paid attention to air-raid security. Why should planes drop bombs on Cannes? Later, under Vichy insistence, some housewives had had old curtains dyed black. Now that it was a question of being shot at, they took the problem more seriously.

Every house had shutters. Those with solid ones were safe. People with slatted ones soon discovered how to plug up the open spaces with twisted newspaper. A hot airless room was better than bullets. There was still the risk that the shutters were not tight at the hinges. Children were warned to fling themselves flat on the floor at the first ping.

So far, no one had been seriously injured. There were times when shooting was heard. In the morning a riddled cat might be found—although cats were a great rarity by this time—or an office would be found in shambles: splintered glass, rubble, potholes. All because an office boy or a cleaning woman had been careless.

The full weight of the German changeover fell on Frank's shoulders. Fortunately, not many airmen were coming through. When they did, Frank did not hesitate. He was like a cat at night. But everyone knew what the Germans do to cats.

Letty asked nothing better than to stay at home behind high walls. René held a different view. As a neutral and a rich woman, he thought, she should be seen at the Carlton. The Germans respected money and were less suspicious of rich people and familiar faces. René did not need to remind her that, for the moment, the Carlton was the only place which still managed to get black-market food.

Mary Fowler was having drinks at her usual table. Her entourage had not changed except for the uniforms of the officers. She did not seem surprised to see Letty; she even nodded in greeting.

"Why does she take my presence in Cannes for granted?" Letty asked René.

"I fixed that ages ago," he said, "when she asked where poor Letty was going. I got it out of her first that she knew nothing whatsoever about your passport."

Later on, during the meat course, Letty complained that the food stuck in her throat each time she looked up and saw a German uniform.

"Never mind," said René, "you are behaving beautifully. As cool as an oyster on a bed of ice."

"Rather what I feel like," she said, "about to be forked into someone's mouth."

Letty's Carlton appearances paid off almost at once. Frank had had a few hours' notice from his policeman that German officers were going the rounds of large villas with the object of requisitioning them for the army. By sheer luck, there was no one in the garage-house.

Letty prepared for them by stripping off her garden slacks and dressing the part of a femme du monde. René came up posthaste, bringing extra ration cards, the proof, he told her, that the house was jam-packed with people. He poured out a stiff brandy for himself and Letty. He knew that she became more and more dignified the more she drank. While they waited René said again that Letty should stand on her rights; the Germans had no business to requisition property belonging to a neutral.

"There is nothing to worry about," he said once more in a vain effort to calm himself about the wireless upstairs. It was too big and too late to try to hide it. As though making for the bathroom, he went up to Letty's room. He closed the doors of the cabinet, flung a silk scarf over it, and placed a rather lovely Lalique jar on top.

Letty had had three brandies by the time the gate bell rang. She moved down the drive with her keys, a queen bearing the insignia of state. She opened the gate wide and René saw an officer salute, and then half bow over her hand. A short conversation followed. Letty shut the gate on the Germans and started back alone.

René met her halfway. "What happened?"

"He recognized me as the Irish friend of the beautiful Frau Fowler." She reached out and took his arm. "His friendliness was the shock. Took the starch from my bones; they are like string."

He sat her down in a comfortable chair and brought her another drink. Presently he said, "Now that that is that and we have a little time in front of us, with your permission and Frank's help, I propose to store the pictures in the attic."

To his surprise, Letty agreed. "That officer told me that the Gestapo are arriving in ten days, and that they are not as kind as the SS. He is SS, by the way. Was he warning me? Or just talking, boasting, calling the other kettle black? Do you think he could have been drunk?"

"Not as drunk as you are, my dear," said René.

Frank must have been on the lookout somewhere; he joined them at once. When they told him about the Gestapo, he nodded gloomily; he already knew from Jacques. As for the pictures, he suggested that they start now, this minute. "And while we are about it," he said, "we'll put the wireless up there, too. I can rig up a plug in a jiffy."

Now began a time when each individual held his breath and looked over his shoulder. It wasn't the German Gestapo, uniformed and marked by speech, that unnerved the people as much as the plain-clothes Frenchmen who worked for them. They were the ears and eyes; the ones who mingled and sat in the cafés. How could you spot them except that their faces were unfamiliar?

Walking a tightrope in the dark, Nina called it. Friends dropped out of sight. Where to? Into the hands of the Gestapo or safe in the mountains? One could only speculate and pray.

Anyone who reappeared after an interval was avoided like the plague. No matter his trusted position before, now his cronies edged away from him. It was axiomatic: the one path back was as a tool of the enemy.

"And beware of gypsies," Frank said. "Only those who work for Hitler are still at large."

It was a time of rumors, of anonymous letters, of denouncements, and of murder among Frenchmen for material gain or petty jealousy. Letty's and Nina's coiffeur was found shot in the back. A nephew stepped into his shoes and into his shop. The story went round that it was he who contrived the assassination. A schoolboy was shot for wearing a Cross of Lorraine under his shirt, denounced by a schoolfellow. The execution was carried out by a German firing squad in front of the entire school. To set an example, once and for all. The boy behaved with legendary dignity, shouting *Vive la France!* at the last moment. The next morning a fourth of the school had disappeared into nowhere. The example had worked the wrong way round.

On July 10, Sicily was invaded by the Allies. On the twenty-fourth, the Fascist Grand Council, led by Grandi and Ciano, voted to replace Mussolini by a national government under the supreme authority of the king. Badoglio formed a provisional government. Mussolini was arrested and put out of the way on the island of Ponza.

"Thank goodness," it was said in the street, "the Italians have at last piped down."

chapter
fourteen

Italy lost its stature with Mussolini. Unconditional surrender, publicly announced a month and a half later, was a sequel so long expected that it was already old hat. The Allies landed at Taranto and Salerno. Jubilation at the prospect of a rapid takeover of the country died on the beachheads. The German army had anticipated them; it was there and everywhere in control. With the support of naval guns the Allies managed to keep their toehold; and in time and by degrees, they pushed forward. It was the beginning of a long slow slogging-match against German forces and bad weather.

"I don't understand it," Letty said, coming down from her attic listening post. "How can our troops be tied down by rain in southern Italy when snow, ice, and $-50°$ does nothing to hold up the Russians? *They* have the Germans on the run. If we aren't nippy, we'll soon have Russians in our laps."

There was no answer to Letty's statement and no one gave one.

The Great Russian Advance was disquieting to

many people, except of course to rabid communists. Stories had begun to leak out from the Drôme that the Germans were using "brainwashed" Russian POW's to fight the maquisards. The indiscriminate brutality of the Russians made Germans seem model schoolchildren. They drew no line between maquisards and civilians, favoring anyone who possessed an object which caught their fancy: a wristwatch or a bicycle. They may have had no idea where their duties lay, and they spoke only Russian. For them, the easiest way of getting a man off a bicycle was to shoot him.

"How do we know that these stories are true?" Frank said.

"Something must be up," said René. "I know for a fact that the maquis here are depleting their own stock of arms to send them to their comrades there."

True or not, before many months passed, the Germans refused travel permits into the Drôme. It was rumored that the entire département was now in the hands of the maquis.

"Why don't we all go?" said Nina.

"With no trains, roadblocks, German sentries?" Frank said. "I've got my work cut out here."

Indeed he had. He was now getting servicemen who had slipped away from Italian POW camps in the hiatus and confusion of the German seizure of that country. For a short time he had tried using a house in the country near Opio. It had seemed foolish to bring the men into Cannes under Gestapo noses. He soon found out that isolated houses were exactly the targets the Germans had their eyes on. He got his men out by a near squeak and was back again at Letty's. "We had to pull out in daylight," he said. "And men stick out like sore thumbs in open country. It needs a town, a crowd, for the best cover."

"Like a flock for stolen sheep," said René. "An old gag."

For most people 1943-44 was the hardest winter of the war. Hope dangled, tantalizing, an unreachable carrot. Endurance had come to an end. They had all been in need and had gone without for too long. Three quarters of the children had contracted tuberculosis. Clothes were threadbare. Pillage in hotels a commonplace. René came back from the Carlton with extraordinary tales. Not only sheets, towels, and pillowcases disappeared with the transient guest but also rugs and curtains. An inspection of rooms became necessary before suitcases were turned over to the departing guest. Even so, some got away with one sheet by folding the other one double to look like top and bottom.

"Why sheets?" asked Letty.

"Shirts, dresses," René said. "You can dye them."

When René went to Marseilles he found that the hotels there no longer made up beds. If you wanted sheets, you had to bring your own.

And no longer did one get the full food ration. The fault of thieves and outlaws, Vichy proclaimed. Warehouses and local shops were constantly raided by maquisards. How else could they survive? They had forfeited their ration cards.

"It's the same number of people," Nina said, "whether the men are at home or in the wilds. You'd think it would even out."

René laughed at her. "Not if you are huddled on a cold mountainside and have just seized a side of beef. You are going to roast great chunks of it and eat like kings."

The Carlton was often reduced to offering white beans as their black-market dish. Twenty-five beans to a portion. René swore that he always counted them.

Letty had a letter from a young Jewish woman who had been at the Carlton until the total occupation, she and her husband and three small children. The husband had walked across the Pyrénées and she had taken the children to a country estate in the neighborhood of Grenoble. It was a hurriedly scrawled letter telling Letty not to write to the old address. The Germans had come and burned the house down. Luckily she and the children were out walking in the woods at the time. Warned by smoke, they had crept near enough to make out German soldiers against the flames. She had contacts in Grenoble so she was not without money, but no amount of that would replace the children's warm clothes. We cannot live through another winter, she wrote.

A refrain heard on all sides: *not another winter. Something will have to happen.*

"I cannot imagine what *can* happen here in France, can you?" Letty asked her household. "It was touch and go breaking into Italy, and that coast wasn't bristling with blockhouses, mines, and booby traps. Now that we are in, *and* in force, do we move? Like a snail."

Rome was taken by the Allies at the beginning of June.

"Nine months to get from Salerno to Rome," said Letty. "A few hours' drive."

Two days later, on June 6, the English and Americans landed in Normandy: they were on French soil. A great black iron lid had been lifted. Lightheaded, giddy, constricted in the chest, Letty held her breath. Would it work? Could we stand fast? Hold on?

Early and late she was in the attic listening. She couldn't bring herself to go down for meals. Nina took up trays. At last, the Allies broke through the outer wall of German defense and began to fan out inland. A sigh of relief went up through the house. Still, Letty did not appear.

"Battle reports don't come through that often," said René, "nor do they change much in a day." He turned to Nina. "What *is* she doing up there?"

"Listening. To one thing or another. To those code messages for the French: *La Corse ressemble à une poire* sort of thing."

"She'll drive herself dotty," he said.

"I don't think she really hears it," said Nina. "I get the impression that she sits there to be alone."

Several days later when René came to the house for lunch and there was still no sign of Letty, he exploded. "This won't do," he said. "In this weather that place must be like an oven." He jumped to his feet but Nina caught him by the arm.

"Let me, later, after lunch. She's already got her tray, and she's in a strange mood. It will need kid gloves and patience."

When René had gone and the house was empty, Nina locked the door and climbed the stairs. As she stepped up into the attic it was as though a blanket had dropped over her; it was hot, airless, and dark. No wonder Letty told her to leave the tray outside. She waited for her eyes to adjust themselves. At the far end she could make out Letty bending forward toward the low murmur of the machine. When Nina went over to her, without glancing up, she said, "Listen to what I've got on the shortwave." She turned the sound higher. A man's voice came through as clearly as though he were standing beside them. "I've made my way to the east side of the field," he said. "There's a ditch here and I'm standing in it. The tank is beginning to turn. Now the tank is headed east, toward me. I'm standing in a ditch. My God, the tank is coming straight at me. The tank is . . ." Static sputtered and shrieked on and on before Letty switched it off. Presently Letty said, "I didn't know that would happen."

Nina dropped to the floor with her arms across Letty's knees. "Letty, darling, you can't help by listening. Come downstairs. We'll go out in the air. It's stifling here. You are ruining yourself."

"Ruining myself? My dear child, I *am* ruined. They are bringing it with each step forward." She was staring straight ahead at the blank wall, a plaster statue, immobile and stiff.

"It's the heat," Nina said. "I'd be crazy, too, if I stayed up here. Come with me."

"I thought we'd never get out of this in my lifetime. So I began to cheat. I am a cheat and a fraud. A traitor, too, if it comes down to that. Nothing is left: honor, decency, self-respect."

Nina did not speak and Letty went on in the same monotonous tone as though she were talking in her sleep. "How could I? All those checks and I didn't even bother to keep count. What's the use of keeping count if the money is not there?" A brief silence and she said, "When you think that death is being dished out to everybody here and there—that man with the tank—it's incredible that you can't have it for the asking."

"Letty!" Nina was on her feet, shaking her. A minute later her arms were round her. "If it's money, darling, René will fix it. And my mother. Stop worrying. I'm going to tell René."

Letty sprang to life. "Don't. You can't; he is the last person. I couldn't face him; I couldn't see him again. The Germans can hold on for months. We'll need money. A bit more won't make any difference. Let me have a few months. Please. If you promise, I'll come down with you now. Otherwise . . ." Letty didn't finish the sentence.

Nina's dress was sticking to her body and she could feel drops of sweat running down between her breasts. It was a hellhole up here. "All right," she said. "I promise."

They went out into the back garden and Nina pulled two deck chairs into the shade where a slight breeze blew in from the sea. Lying there, Nina looked the more done in of the two. Letty's confession had been a shock, and in some curious way the weight seemed to have been shifted onto her, bound hand and foot to it by her promise.

Letty was reviving. "It's lovely out here," she said. "How right you were, Nina dear, to insist. What a waste not to enjoy what one has."

Nina was trying to muster strength to go inside and wash the luncheon dishes. The next thing she knew she was gazing up through leaves. She'd been asleep; for how long? She turned toward Letty's chair. It was empty. She jumped up and at once saw Letty moving in the vegetable garden; from time to time she would stoop and pull a weed. She's all right for the moment, Nina thought, but will it last? What on earth will happen in the end?

That evening Frank and René brought with them the hideous story of the massacre at Oradour.

No one spoke for a long time.

At last, Letty said, "What in God's name did they do to bring that on themselves?"

"Absolutely nothing," said Frank. "The SS made a mistake. There was another Oradour quite near, Oradour-sur-Vayres. A sniper got a German officer there."

"Criminal to shoot Germans in a village," said René. "Why can't they get out in the open country?"

"They are killing Germans in Nice," Frank said. "The moment they catch one alone in a side street. Afterwards, three hostages are hanged. They do it by the feet now; it takes longer." He spat, the recognized sign of his deepest disgust. He went on, "I've been talking to an agent just out from England. The maquis here were supposed to wait for a particular signal before going into action, but as soon as we landed in Normandy, everybody grabbed arms and started shooting. It means the slaughter of hundreds of innocent victims. Oradour is not the only place where they burn people alive."

René said, "The Germans have lost their heads. They are like mad dogs." He looked at the two women. "Now is the time to stay behind high walls and locked gates."

"What is happening to Mary Fowler?" Letty asked.

"Poor Mary, she spends her time drinking with German officers. She's a fool not to leave at once and go to a place where she's not known. And behave herself."

"Shouldn't you tell her?"

"I did," said René. "She laughed and said that she is too fond of comfort to travel. And that all the good-looking men are here."

Frank said, "I've got a lookout rigged up not far from the front gate. So don't get a fright if you see one of my men. I try to keep someone down there most of the time. If the bell rings and no one is there, for God's sake, climb the ladder and peek through the crotch of the tree. You get a clear view of the other side."

"And if it is the Germans?"

"Scram. Call Nina and bolt through the back gate. I told both of you to keep that key on you. Don't stop to take anything."

"What about you and the men?"

"We all hear the front bell. If I see you tearing back to the house, that's it."

René broke in, "The Germans won't come up here. Who cares about keeping order when his world is crumbling?"

"The Germans might," said Nina.

At that moment the front bell clanged. Frank loped out of the room. They all went to the front door and watched him flitting down through the trees. It was still light enough to see. Halfway, he met a man; they spoke; and Frank turned back. "It's a woman, English-looking, with a suitcase," he told Letty.

"Who could it be?" she said.

"Go and see. If she's English, she shouldn't be out on the streets."

Presently Letty came up the drive carrying the suitcase with a much smaller woman at her side, talking excitedly. As they got nearer René said, "Her friend, Bunny Sutton. I wonder how she got out?"

When they were all in the drawing room, Letty said, "They took the Englishwomen to Paris and kept them in a barracks for a few weeks, then sent them back."

Bunny went into more detail: "We were a present from Vichy to the Germans, but they didn't want us. There was no place to put us: the women's camps were already overcrowded. In the end, they sent us back where we came from and held us under *résidence forcée*. That meant Cavaillon for me."

"What about the men?" René asked. "I haven't heard a word from any of them."

"In the camp at St. Denis."

"But why are you *here*?" said Letty.

"We got another order, this time to move farther inland, with five départements to choose from including the Drôme. Obviously the order was way out-of-date, but it meant that we should leave Cavaillon. We weren't told to report to the police anywhere. A man I knew was bringing black-market stuff to Cannes and offered me a lift. He knew I had a house here."

"What happened to it?" Letty asked.

"The house is all right. I made one of those deals with an English friend married to a Frenchman. I went there and she wouldn't let me in. Said it was dangerous. She didn't even unlock the gate."

Frank said, "Cannes is full of Germans, and we've got the Gestapo."

"So is Cavaillon," said Bunny, "and they ordered us out."

Letty looked at Frank who was at one side and slightly behind Bunny. He shook his head.

René saw the exchange and at once proposed that Bunny stay in Letty's small house. He turned to Bunny and said, "The garden is not overlooked. And if you promise not to go down into Cannes, I'll see that you have provisions."

"I'll promise anything for a roof and a bed," said Bunny. She looked it, too; quite suddenly her exhaustion was visible.

"You'll sleep here tonight," Letty said, not looking at Frank. "What about something to eat first?"

Bunny shook her head. "I'm too tired for that," she said.

Letty led her off upstairs. Just before they all sat down to dinner she went up again with a bowl of hot soup. As she came back into the dining room René was saying, "You see, the Germans no longer keep up with their administrative duties."

"She'll eat the soup," said Letty. "What took the stuffing out of her was that business about her house."

"When the war is over," said Frank, "something will have to be done about all those phony sales. People are so greedy that no one can trust his best friend." With that, he was off on the subject of human nature.

Letty interrupted. "For heaven's sake, talk about something pleasant."

chapter
fifteen

Summer had not been as hot since 1940—invasion
weather, René called it, and thanked God that this time
he was not plodding down the long length of France on
foot. It was too hot to move. They lay in deck chairs in
the shade at the back of the house. Overhead, Allied
planes crisscrossed high in the white sky, thickening the
heat with their vibration. They listened for where the
bombs would drop, mostly distant booms, and Frank
would guess at the target. Once in a while one came close
enough to rip the air and blaze the darkness inside their
skulls.

After the inexplicable raid on Marseilles, when
bombs were dribbled along the Canebière and nowhere
else, Frank and René hacked a shallow trench in the
olive grove. "The Americans fly too high to gauge what
they'll hit," Frank said. The Marseilles raid stirred up a
lot of resentment: against the Allies, of course, and
against the Germans who refused to move the rubble from

the bodies and refused to allow the municipality to organize work parties. Rumor gave the dead as three thousand.

"Do you think they are going to land on this coast?" Letty asked.

"Sure to," said Frank.

There did not seem much point in hoeing and weeding a garden that might soon go up in smoke. In any case, Letty did not want to go that far from the others. It was a source of comfort, being together.

"This curious semi-paralysis reminds me," René said, "of the first time I was attacked by a Stuka. It was early, just beginning to be light, and I was shaving. It dived straight down at me, screaming. I couldn't move to save myself. I went on shaving, slow-motion. Afterwards the captain harangued me for trying to show off."

"We're being reasonable," said Frank. "It's asking for trouble to show ourselves outside."

"If only we had some sort of idea of what's in store." Letty spoke, gazing up at the sky.

"God forbid," said Frank.

There were no more cigarettes, but René had managed to get hold of some dried tobacco leaves. For hours on end Letty snipped these leaves into threads with a pair of fine cuticle scissors. When she had made a pile she rolled cigarettes with a small metal contraption for that purpose. "I shall never pity factory workers again," she said. "Mechanical work is soothing. One's mind becomes a blank. One doesn't think of anything."

Frank followed Nina when she went into the kitchen and stood there, fiddling with things. "I'm worried about Letty," he said at last. "If she only *would* keep her mind a blank! It lurches about as though she'd lost her rudder. Yesterday she cornered me about white butterflies. It wouldn't mean a thing to you," he said to Nina. "You haven't been sailing here in the autumn. From September on we used to meet batches of them out at sea, flying toward the horizon. We could never figure out where they were headed for. Now, she maintains it was mass suicide, a glorious end. 'They've had their day,' she said, 'and they know it. They don't wait to be shriveled by long cold nights.'"

Frank paused. "She talked wild and high and sort of involved. Is she just crazy or has she some mad idea of swimming out? What do you think?"

He did not wait for an answer. "Everything now is coming our way; so she must be cracked." He started for the door. "I thought you ought to be warned," he said. "Butterflies," he muttered, *"Butterflies."*

Every Frenchman knew that Paris was mined, and that Hitler had sworn never to surrender it except in ruins. Now that the BBC had announced that American troops were on the outskirts of Chartres, René and Nina pulled their chairs closer together. The parents of both of them lived in the same apartment house on the Ile St. Louis, a circumstance which had brought them together in early childhood.

"All the bridges will be blown and the Cité."

"We are next to a bridge."

"I'm not worried about our families," René said. "They can get out if they want to."

"Mother wouldn't go. I know she wouldn't."

"It's Paris. Nothing in the world will be the same without Paris."

Letty suspended her tobacco-snipping. "Will anything be the same, anyway?" she asked.

A courier came to the gate with a message for Frank. Whatever it was, he kept it to himself. That evening he told them that he wouldn't be in much for the next few days and he would no longer be using the garage; so if Letty wanted her English friend to come up to the house, it was all right with him.

"Do bring her up," said René. "Taking provisions down there is like getting in with a tiger. She's scatty with loneliness." He turned to Frank. "Don't forget I'm a good man in a pinch."

Frank nodded and said he wouldn't forget. He walked over to his quarters. No one heard or saw him leave.

Bunny talked like a waterfall at first and then she settled down to the deck-chair life and desultory remarks. At midday René went up to the attic with Letty to listen to the BBC. They came down again almost at once; no news, the electricity was off. Bunny said that she'd often thought it strange there weren't more cuts during a war. Then Nina came out from the kitchen saying she couldn't make lunch without water. The taps didn't run.

"We must get water from somewhere," Nina said.

"There's one of those round *bassin* reservoirs down at my house," said Letty.

Nina fetched a bucket and a tall metal jug and held them out to René. "Too bad Frank isn't here," he said, taking them.

He spent the best part of the afternoon filling up the three bathtubs in the house and the one out in Frank's quarters. He told the women that that was half their total supply and should be used sparingly in case this thing went on for some time. He was going down into Cannes to see what he could find out.

The streets were empty except for a straggling line of children at the three or four public pumps which, surprisingly enough, gave forth water. It was late in the afternoon and the children looked as though they had been standing there for hours. Suddenly something snapped. The boy at the pump gave the handle a vicious spin and with the palm of his hand sprayed the queue behind. The line broke and the battle was on: the tussle for the pump, and water shooting in every direction. René retreated and tried the likely cafés. No one he knew. He walked on to a friend's flat and knocked but got no answer. He turned back and let himself into his own flat. Quickly he tried the taps and the light. Neither worked. He didn't linger, anxious not to be caught there. Once again out on the Croisette, he saw by the sun that it was time to go back up the hill. Without electricity, they would have to eat while it was still daylight.

They all helped carry dishes out to the kitchen and stacked them. The light was going fast now. Bunny hurried off upstairs, saying she wasn't familiar enough with the house to go to bed in the dark.

"Just beginning to get cool," said René.

"I don't mind *feeling* my way to bed," Nina said.

"May we?" René asked Letty, picking up two bottles of red wine from the rack. Nina took glasses and they started out the back way to the chairs. They hadn't settled themselves when Letty joined them, bottle in one hand, glass in the other. "I couldn't face upstairs," she said. "Not when I'm this wide-awake."

Nothing could have been more reasonable and yet Nina wondered. Was Letty afraid of what she might say to René, sitting in the dark drinking wine? Perhaps Letty had even sensed her intention. Because, on the spur of the moment, she had made up her mind to break the promise and speak. The end was upon them; and too much was at stake.

They did not talk much. The thrumming of cicadas filled the night air, blotting out the fainter drone of planes. When the wine had long been drunk Nina, who had night eyes, took the lead. Holding hands didn't work since they fanned out too wide; then René proposed hands on shoulders, prison-fashion. They progressed in this way between bouts of laughter, Nina shushing them because of Bunny. As soon as they touched the stair banister it was plain sailing.

On the day after, while the others were stacking the dinner dishes, René took wine and glasses outside; sitting together in the darkness had become accepted routine.

Frank looked in the next morning to warn them to pay no attention to the rumor that the Germans were gone. True, there were none to be seen. They played this cat-and-mouse game in other places; the moment the populace came out to celebrate, they pounced.

Two days later when they were settled in deck chairs for the afternoon, Frank was suddenly there, standing above them. "This is it," he said. "This morning at eight o'clock the Americans landed down the coast."

"Where?" they cried, jumping up.

"St. Raphaël, Ste. Maxime, a number of places."

"Are you sure?"

"An FFI* got through on a motorbike. The Americans are striking inland, away from us. So sit tight."

"We can't sit tight without water," said René.

"We've put engineers on to it. The Germans wrecked that when they left."

"So they *have* gone?"

"We don't know where to, or how far."

"At least I can go down for food."

"You won't find any. Stocks have been burned; everything the Germans couldn't take."

"What do the people do?"

"They wait," said Frank. "What else?"

Waiting was different now; it was no longer possible to lie flat in deck chairs. Perhaps they were already free? Or were the Germans between them and the Americans? And would they fall back and defend Cannes? If this happened, should they go to the cellar or to the outside trench? They talked and talked and forgot to decide.

Letty thought of John's binoculars. She tried the

* Forces françaises de l'intérieur—the resistance force controlled by de Gaulle.

upper windows and the terrace, but from nowhere could she get a glimpse of the coast road. This war had been like that from the beginning; she had never been able to see ahead of time what was going to come.

Suddenly the front bell rang out. The color left Letty's face. "If that is the Germans now!" she said. René held out his hand for the key. He ran to Frank's lookout and waved reassurance before he opened the gate. Frank pushed his bicycle-cart through.

"He never comes that way," said Letty.

"He'd have to with that cart."

Frank looked bad-tempered and he came up to them grumbling. "The idiot wouldn't leave until he saw me start out with my truck. He wanted to see Madame Bunny, but I told him I'd dump the cases in the sea if he tried to follow." He handed Bunny a letter. "The fellow said he got through from Cavaillon the back way on mountain roads without running into American troops. If that's true, Collabos will be escaping into Italy." Frank jumped on the bicycle and went shooting down the drive. René shut and locked the gate after him.

Bunny was staring at the two suitcases. "Those aren't mine," she said.

"Why don't you open the letter?" Letty suggested.

Bunny shuffled through the pages until she came to the signature. "It's from Louis, the man who drove me here," she said. "I did leave some things behind, sheets and things."

Letty picked up one of the cases. "Could be sheets," she said, feeling the weight.

By this time René had joined them. He carried the

cases into the house and was back at once. He had put them in Bunny's room, and now he was going down to have a look at Cannes. If Frank was as busy as he said, there must be something cooking.

Bunny disappeared into the house with her unread letter. Letty and Nina discussed the problem of dinner. All they had to eat was tomatoes, onions, garlic, and olive oil. Not a scrap of anything else. For days now Nina had produced a surprising range of menus within that strait jacket. Tonight she proposed baked onions masked in a thick tomato sauce.

Letty picked the tomatoes before she went up to her room. Bunny was sitting at the top of the stairs, apparently waiting for her. She stood up and began speaking at once. "It wasn't sheets," she said. "Something I have to keep for Louis. I'll need a safe place. He thought I'd be in my own house, you see. Here, I don't know."

"Your room is as safe as anywhere," said Letty. "You can lock the door if you like."

"Anyone can break a door open."

Letty looked down at her in surprise. "Why should they?"

"Louis wrote that he'd left such a trail trying to find me that anyone could trace the cases. He said that there was a chance and to be careful."

"What on earth is it? And who is anyone?"

"It's just money, stacks of it," said Bunny, "so much it scares me. And anyone is anyone who knew he had it, I suppose."

Letty was silent for a few minutes and then she said that whenever it was a question of hiding something, she invariably thought of *The Purloined Letter*. There was an entire cupboard filled with empty suitcases belonging to John and Laura. If she were Bunny, she would take two of the heavy bottom cases, pack the money into them, and arrange them again under the others. As for Louis' cases, she would fill them from the linen cupboard and leave them in her room. "Come along and I'll help," said Letty.

When Bunny emptied out the first case of bank notes Letty sat back on her heels and said, "Your friend Louis must have had a pretty thick mattress."

Bunny didn't get it and made no answer.

"Isn't it rather extraordinary," Letty went on, "for a Frenchman to leave this with a virtual stranger and a foreigner to boot?"

"I'm not a stranger," Bunny said. "We saw a lot of each other in Cavaillon. And what's more, he says it's safer because I *am* English."

"You'd think he'd hold on to it."

"How can he, when he's off to the mountains?"

"You've read it wrong. They're coming down from the mountains now."

Bunny didn't say anything. She was absorbed in re-packing the bundles.

Letty stared at her with growing astonishment. "Do you mean to say that he is a pro-German?"

"I said no such thing. I happen to know that he hates Germans. He got his own back by making them pay through the nose for everything."

"*He collaborated?*" Letty said.

"Call it what you like; the result is what counts. He was left in control and was able to hold back a certain share of his crops for the French market. The others could not do that."

"Are you sure he isn't trying to whitewash himself?"

Bunny was indignant. "I saw how it worked out; I was there for more than a year."

"I suppose," said Letty, "that everyone—Hitler, quislings, the lot—can find a plausible excuse for his own behavior."

Bunny was about to protest when she saw that Letty was restacking the luggage cupboard in the way she had suggested. René's voice was heard below. Quickly now Letty filled Louis' cases from the back of the linen cupboard, handed them to Bunny, and went downstairs.

René was telling Nina about Cannes. As though the plague had hit it: streets deserted, shops and houses shuttered. Frank wasn't at his place. He had walked on as far as the Carlton, and there he found the doors locked. Georges let him in when he went on knocking. A few of the guests were sitting round playing cards. At the desk he was told that Mary Fowler had checked out days before. He went through to the kitchens and talked to the chef. All he could get out of him was a chunk of yesterday's national bread and a stream of profanity: how in the devil could he work with no materials, no water, and no light?

Nina was delighted with the bread. "At least it's something solid."

René made a face. "As solid as a brick," he said.

chapter
sixteen

It is axiomatic that when things start happening, they happen all together and at the same time. During that night the household was awakened by loud knockings and grumblings in the pipes. Then Letty heard the rush of water and made her way to the bathroom. As soon as she'd turned the taps off, lights sprang on all over the house. The fear of showing a light was so ingrained that she began to run. She met Nina head-on at the top of the stairs and they rushed down together. When the house was dark again, Nina went over to see to the taps in the garage-house. Letty waited for her at the kitchen door. It seemed a long time.

She came back breathless. "Frank was there," she said. "Just got in." Half-pushing, half-leading, Nina bundled Letty into the storeroom, which had no window, and snapped on the light. "It's too important to tell you in the dark," she said. "The Americans have come. The Americans are in Cannes."

Letty could not remember whether she had gone to sleep again for the rest of the night. She was alone for breakfast and couldn't imagine what the others were doing until she saw how late it was. She toasted a slice of the bread René had brought and went through the motions of eating it. She felt unreal and the toast was unreal and then René came down from the attic where he'd been listening to the BBC. It would seem that the people of Paris had liberated themselves. Barricades, street fighting, and all. *Paris had not been blown up.*

He danced off to find Nina.

She was in the back among the oleander bushes. From time to time she snipped off a dead blossom. She was doing it at random, a snip here, a snip there. René recognized the signs: she was brooding. "What a way to celebrate," he called out. She turned and gave him a rather weak smile. "It's all right," he said, and he told her about Paris.

She brightened but the brightness was clouded. "I'm worried about Letty," she said. "She's taken the tube of Veronal from the medicine cupboard."

"Vidal gave it for bombings. These last days we've expected worse."

"I've been watching it," said Nina, "and she took it last night *after she knew*."

"What's up, then?"

"All those checks. She hasn't got the money."

"That! I knew that all along; it stuck out a mile."

"You should have said something. It's you she minds about most."

"Said something?" René looked exasperated. "Every time I brought up the subject, she shied and practically ran from the room."

Nina said, "We'll have to act quickly. Get hold of that tube."

"It's too absurd," René said. "Do you think I would just let things get out of hand like that? After all, I am fond of Letty. I must say in her defense that she isn't a businesswoman. She has never once asked me about her money from the stove shares. That started coming in early on, before it was clear which way the war would turn. I was able to buy up good investments for her, things that will make a mint as soon as the war is over, like brick factories and cement works closed for the duration."

"You mean that she will be all right?" Nina threw herself on René and he didn't know whether she was hugging or shaking him. "She ought to be told at once."

"Not by me," he said. "*You* tell her. Just give the facts. Don't say I've got her covered. Tell her she'll be rich after the war."

"How can I?" Nina wailed. "I promised not to talk to you about money."

"Tell her I talked. Say I boasted about the investments."

"I've got to collect myself," she said. She looked round, saw a stone bench and sat down. Presently she looked up at him. "If those checks go to her English bank, I don't see what good it does to own brick factories in France that have not begun to earn money."

René sat down beside her. "I've tried to get round that," he said. "Most of the checks are held by the Syndicate. I've made a deal with them to redeem the checks here in France in French francs at the then current rate of exchange. I won't budge, of course, until normal banking is re-established between the two countries. I have to take the chance that that will give us enough time."

"You *are* an angel," she said, brushing a light kiss across his cheek. She took a few steps toward the house and then came back. "She's awfully moral and naïve. I think she believes that she has done wrong and should be punished."

"Don't give it a thought," said René. He stretched his legs straight out and thrust his hands in his pockets, sliding down to rest on his back. A splash of sun hit him across the face, showing up the deep lines. "If anyone has managed to scrape through these years in France and has kept a moral to bless himself with, I'll eat my hat."

"You haven't got a hat."

As she moved off slowly toward the house René called after her that he was going down to watch the fireworks. He did not much want to go but he didn't want Letty to run out to him until she'd had time to simmer down.

Frank and René came back together in the late afternoon. Frank was in high spirits. "The Liberation Committee has appointed a new mayor," he said. "Our friend Jacques is chief of police. They've sent out *camions* to collect food wherever there is any. They think they're practicing communism but it's just common sense."

René had seen another side; he'd been with the FFI. They had caught a hall full of Miliciens* and Collabos and were knocking the hell out of them. Tomorrow was to be the public executions. A slight twitch like a shiver went through him. He said, "They've already started shaving the women. Put them up on stands in the market place so everyone could see and then marched them through the streets. It wasn't pretty."

"You've got to allow for a bit of that," said Frank. "They have to clear up the mess; make a clean sweep."

"It wasn't clean," René said, "and I'm sick of thugs."

"I do agree," Bunny joined in. "They don't take into account . . ."

Frank gave her a sardonic glance that made Letty wonder if he'd found out about her friend Louis. When Frank spoke it was to Letty. He told her that the American captain was astonished to hear that there were Englishwomen in Cannes and begged for the honor of having lunch with them the next day.

This brought a howl from Nina. "How could you! We've nothing to eat."

"He's sending his driver up with army food. His lieutenant is coming to lunch, too."

"What are they like, the Americans?" Letty asked.

Frank said, "The captain is very young, very tired, a dedicated soldier."

"The GI's," said René, "are like a pack of St. Bernard puppies, handing out goodies and wanting to play."

* Men picked by Darnand in January 1943 to work in co-operation with the Gestapo, Waffen SS and other German forces of repression. Loosely called "the French Gestapo."

"*Play?*" said Nina.

René grinned at her. "With little girls like you."

Afterwards, Letty was glad the captain and lieutenant had come. It put a seal on the fact of liberation. At the beginning when she thought it was going to be sticky—the officers came in awkward and stiff—she pushed a glass of champagne into their hands at once. The young captain looked happier when he spotted Nina and the lieutenant, a much older man, drifted to her side with every appearance of pleasure. By the second glass he was making her laugh. He argued that she couldn't possibly stay behind in this God-forsaken country full of foreigners. She must come with them in their tanks. They were pushing on that very afternoon.

Several times conversation was interrupted by delegations from Cannes, red-faced men in hard collars and dark suits, bearing choice bottles, to welcome the Americans. Each time, the bottles had to be opened and toasts drunk. For Letty the party took on a euphoric haze that did nothing to dim the official aspect, some of the glory of which she knew was being rubbed off on her as hostess.

At one o'clock the driver, who had been standing at rigid attention against the wall, announced that lunch was served. And, indeed it was—by him.

Letty was seduced by a delicious meat loaf which the Americans shunned. "We've seen too much of that," they said, and fell upon the tomato salad and green beans Nina had got from Juanito. The Americans ate fast and gulped their coffee. Letty couldn't get over the fact that it was real coffee. "Not to me," the lieutenant said. "It's Nes, a kind of powder."

The captain collected his snapshots from Nina and said it was time. The lieutenant turned to Letty. Was she sure she wouldn't change her mind and come along? Then they were in the jeep and waving all the way down the drive.

Bunny had begged off the luncheon party. You don't want an extra woman, she had said. "And besides, I don't get on with Americans. My sister married one." Letty did not try to persuade her. For the past week she'd been positively mousy; come and gone without a word. Is it lack of nourishment, Letty wondered? But as far as that went, they were all in the same boat. She toyed with the idea of suggesting a hotel. Any danger to Bunny was over now and she had plenty of money. The thought of the suitcases made Letty pause; she liked knowing that that much cash was in the house. Bunny would have to stay.

"Where is Bunny?" Letty said, linking arms with Nina as they turned away from the now empty drive.

"Out. To see her lawyer, I think."

"Give her a slice of that meat loaf when she comes in."

"Wasn't it fun?" said Nina. She smiled up at Letty and Letty returned it with a conspiratorial gleam. How she has come to life again, Nina thought.

They went through to the kitchen to tackle the aftermath of a luncheon party; to their surprise everything had been left in admirable order. On the corner of the sideboard was a neat stack of objects: packages of American cigarettes, tins of Nescafé, chewing gum, lemon crystals, powder to disinfect water. Nina explained that army food came in cartons which contained all these extras. She'd watched the cook open them with amazement.

Letty picked up the cigarettes and said that Nina could have the chocolate. "We'll share out the coffee." She pried off the top of a coffee tin and sniffed. "Let's make a cup now," she said and chose a cigarette called "Lucky Strike" because the name was appropriate. Nina put the water on to boil.

Letty inhaled deeply. "I'm glad you told me about René's investments when you did," she said.

"So am I," Nina answered rather grimly.

"I haven't had a chance to talk to him since then. I'm afraid I'll give myself away; it means so much. And yet I'd like him to know what a difference it makes; how grateful I am."

"Why don't you tell him the truth?"

"The Truth?" said Letty, and was silent. Presently she said, "Yes, I suppose one could. Now that it is over; now that there *is* money. Isn't it odd that the subject of money is taboo unless you have it? It is only the rich who say they can't afford this or that. The poor are silent. It's not logical. I don't understand it."

"I remember what it was like at the pension," Nina said. "If you have no money and say so, people think you are begging. I couldn't speak until I heard about the British allowance."

René poked his head in at the kitchen door. "I smell coffee," he said, and seeing their cups, came in and sat down. Nina got up and made a cup for him, and then, not to leave them in too obvious a fashion, she picked up a garden basket and went out the back way.

The sun was still very hot so she only went as far as the deck chairs. She could hear a mumble of voices but not what was being said. She prayed that Letty would have the courage. After some time she heard them laughing. At least that meant that they were relaxed and at ease alone together, something they hadn't been for a long time.

With an effort she got up and walked toward the vegetable garden. Could they or could they not face more tomatoes? She decided it wasn't necessary as she had kept back a modest pile of green beans. She went on to look at the artichoke bed, a daily pilgrimage since she'd noticed that small ones had formed. She was bending over, picking off snails, when she felt a smart tap on her behind. She jumped in spite of knowing it must be René. "Little Miss Fix-it," he said. "Thank God, it's all out in the open now." He put an arm round her and gazed down at an artichoke. "That one is almost big enough," he said.

"I've been thinking," Nina said. "Letty would never have written those checks if you hadn't made it so easy and encouraged her all the time. It is your fault, really."

"I know," he said. "She's much too honest. She had been so kind to you, and I wanted you both to have things." René spoke slowly with pauses between sentences. "At first, I thought none of us would survive. Then, when I saw how things were going, I knew it was up to me. A chance in a million, but it will work."

"You were very clever."

"The situation played into my hand."

"Can't I say you were clever to see it?"

"Let's not say anything," said René, "just be grateful . . . well, for *extraordinary* luck."

That night on the way to bed Letty drew Nina into her room. "I've got to talk about it," she said. "It will help me to take it in. It's hard to believe. René says I can pay up, and go on from there. The money will keep on coming in and I shall be rich. Do you realize what that means?"

Nina shook her head.

"I shall have a new life. No more castoff clothes and tarnished handbags. I won't be obliged to pass sandwiches and smile all the time. I can be myself. Stand on my own feet and pay my way. No more poor-relation stuff for me. I spit on it!"

"Darling!" said Nina, laughing. And she went on laughing at the play of expression on Letty's face: disgust, bliss, and mischief were plainly there, superimposed, each struggling for the upper hand. "Darling, how fierce you sound. Not at all like yourself."

Mischief was on top now. "I told you," Letty said, "I told you I am a new self. And won't we have a lovely time! You will stay with me, won't you, until you and René marry?"

"*Yes, please yes!*" said Nina. "You are my family, you and Frank and René. How could I run off?"

"What about your mother?"

"My mother has her own brood with my stepfather. They'll be happy enough without the hybrid foreigner. These war years have brought out my English side; haven't you noticed?"

Letty laughed now because she had lost any sense of nationality in Nina, whom she knew so well. "We've changed places then," she said. "I'm beginning to feel French, the mean kind of French; I find I *calculate*."

"*Idiot*, since the last five hours!" said Nina, and kissed her good-night in the French way, on both cheeks.

chapter
seventeen

The first frenzy of vengeance—the shootings and shavings and manhandlings—spent itself within a month. During that time Nina and Letty kept strictly to the house; they did not want any part of it. They could do without public roistering. It was enough, as Letty said, to wake up each morning with the blessed relief of knowing that the Germans were gone and gone for good.

The cold weather closing in jolted people into facing the fact that the war was not over and that it could not end that winter. The food situation was worse than ever. How could it be otherwise? The Germans had burned the stocks, and the Allies were fully engaged in carrying on the war. If food existed in remote parts of France, there was no way of transporting it: no rolling stock for the railways, no petrol for the roads, the bridges had been blown. You were stuck where you stood and you could buy nothing: no fuel, no clothes, no shoes.

A ray flickered for live-wires in the South. The black market there had taken on a new dimension. Marseilles was being used as a great supply port for the American army. A continuous line of trucks carried goods north. The GI driver and his mate who were fed up and tempted to go AWOL found every inducement to do so *and* money in their pockets. Black marketeers would take over their truck with contents (never disclosed) for the established rate of ten thousand francs. The price was absurdly cheap but it was sufficient to keep two men holed-up and drunk long enough to forget the war. For the marketeers it was a gamble: the truck had to be jettisoned at once, it was too hot to hold—only the contents counted and that might be anything. Sugar or cigarettes were the most prized; K rations brought a high profit; nobody sneezed at a load of good strong boots.

René, of course, had the contacts and the mobility to keep the house on the hill from hunger. At first he used his *gazogène* truck, and then he made friends with some RAF ground staff. He brought them to the house to see Letty who asked nothing better than talking to Englishmen. They enjoyed sitting in a real house, drinking tea, and playing the gramophone. It didn't seem to matter whether it was classical music or dance records. They brought their own tea rations with them and insisted upon brewing it themselves. We like it black, they told Nina, and we have to skim the ants off. The tea, already mixed with sugar, attracted ants. "It's done that way now to save on sugar; it's not half sweet enough." Letty gave them a large sack of sugar the town major had sent her. "We don't touch it," she said, "we're not used to it any more."

They came to the house whenever they got leave, and sometimes when they didn't, Letty suspected. One day they appeared in working overalls with a lorry of assorted tools, oil, and aviation petrol. "We're going to fix up that Bentley," they said, moving toward the garage. The next few days they drank their tea out there. When the job was finished, they took Letty and Nina for a swift silent drive through Cannes to Nice and back again. Letty had forgotten the exhilaration of silky speed; she exclaimed with pleasure.

"We'll keep your tank filled up," they promised.

"None of us would dare take it out." She sounded sad. "The Americans, the English, the FFI, they'd all scramble to requisition it before we'd gone a mile." Back at their lorry, the men dug out some RAF stickers and slapped one on the windscreen and one on the back window. "Don't hang round too many brass hats, that's all."

And so René began using the Bentley for his Marseilles foraging; instead of taking two days, he could go and come back in one. Letty protested at first: John might walk in any day. He was something in the War Office but he could take it into his head to wangle a staff job. René stuck to his guns: John would be delighted to find he still had a car, and doubly delighted that it was in working order. Letty was aware that René carried a loaded revolver on these trips; now he was explicit. "There is a lot of fascist riffraff in the mountains; and since it's turned cold, they're like wolves. I'm damned glad to have a bit of speed behind me."

Once in a while the town major came up to call on Letty, his excuse being that it was restful to get away from military hullabaloo. He liked to sit quietly in the drawing room, sip bourbon (which he brought himself), and talk. He was a Virginian and proud of it, a professional soldier and proud of that, too. He was following in his grandfather's footsteps, a famous general in the American Civil War. It was a name Letty had never heard but she accepted it with a polite, knowing look. He spoke with bitterness of the northern states. Letty found it confusing that he should feel like that and yet fight under the northern flag—she was rather proud of remembering that much of American affairs.

"It's the only flag we've got and the only army. My father stood aloof; it was nearer him. When I was quite young I made the decision to be a realist and to compromise. How else could I make my way?"

The major was again in the drawing room at the time that the scandal broke about the convoy of empty American trucks found in the back country. Letty was up in arms about it. The American was unperturbed. "We've reckoned on it," he said. "We figured out that what with the gangsters in Marseilles and their counterparts in our army, we could count on losing about twenty-five percent of our stuff. Up till now," he went on with a slow smile, "our losses fall short of the estimate."

This relieved Letty's mind immensely. Each time she'd opened a carton of K rations she had felt guilty of weakening the battlefront by that much. But if it were already accounted for! She told her household the good news.

.   .   .

Letty's household was not representative. The general temper of the French was low: they were cold, they were hungry, and nothing was turning out as they had hoped. The central government in Paris was tackling all the wrong problems; they were dampening down the Liberation Committees and routing out communists from local municipal posts. The trials of the collaborators got hung up on legal points or fizzled out when witnesses were forthcoming to say that the man in the dock had saved the life of a Jew and had been pro-English under the skin. The return of French prisoners of war seemed too remote to count on. The new world had not come; the old one was sliding back.

Even the shorn ladies had somehow procured beautiful wigs and were flourishing, this time under the unofficial aegis of the American army. And who could blame the GI's? They didn't know what the wig meant even if they found out that it was one. After all, these women had had a good war; they had kept their sparkle and their smiles. They were gay and ready for a lark.

Life was expensive; prices had again shot up, a natural result of scarcity. Letty was delighted to be able to afford it. René was now handing over the dividends from the stove company, which had swollen beyond belief. The company continued to expand and to work to full capacity. Sawdust stoves were the one remaining source of heat.

Frank began to talk of buying a big boat. "There'll be four cabins, just right for us to sail away in." And no one, save Bunny, noticed that she had not been included. René said, "We'll make a packet this year and the next, but after that. . . ." "It will be enough," said Frank and went off humming to himself rather like a bee.

Several times when they found themselves alone Letty got René to tell her again the ins and outs of her investments and the arrangements he'd made with the Syndicate. She listened as though she were hearing it for the first time. "It's a conjuring trick, making money," she said. "I wish I'd known about it years ago."

"*Dear* Letty!" he said, embracing her. It was too much to explain that the situation had been unique; that it had taken a multitude of circumstances falling just so. A concatenation of circumstances—what a word!

"A penny," she said.

He was glad to be able to beg off by saying "the English language."

Cannes had been made a convalescent center, a play-ground for those in the final stages of recovery, and thus the springboard back to the front lines. It had been that for the Germans, too, after total occupation. But now the inhabitants were brought into the fun. Letty and Nina and Bunny stood the pace for some time; they looked at the snapshots of families and girl friends, they listened, and they drank. It was the drink that got them down. The GI's wouldn't hear of anything less than hard spirits. "Come on, don't be wet. We're having a ball." In the end the women found it wiser to stay at home. When the GI's appeared at the house, they were received with open arms and a loaded drink tray. Slightly apart was a whisky bottle of cold tea. After a while the old friends were gone and newcomers didn't know the way.

The original group of RAF men kept the house humming. They had a way of hopping planes from the far corners of France: a couple of hours, "a piece of cake." And then they began bringing to Letty any of their men who were starting a bout of malaria. Letty was alarmed the first time she saw such a case. She thought the man was dying, he looked so far gone, and shaking. "It's nothing," the man who supported him said. "Bed and quinine. He'll be right as rain in a few days."

The whole lot of them had got it in Egypt and it kept coming back. The men seemed to think that it was brought on again and again by the bitter cold in the North and the fact that their base was makeshift and drafty. "The very devil when you begin to shiver."

Frank and Nina set up a malaria ward in the garage-house and Letty got an order from the town major for the medicines and rations. That winter three to six beds were continually occupied. Letty was glad she'd been given this distraction and interest. She didn't know how she would have got through those long months twiddling her thumbs. She'd had no time to mope over the Battle of the Bulge or, indeed, to hold her breath at the spring advance and the race across the Rhine.

Nina was kept pretty busy in the kitchen and so the job of looking after the men on leave fell to Bunny. Letty was surprised to see how well she did it. Left on her own with a group of men, she blossomed forth. She had them vying with each other for her favors. They played dance records now and Bunny was never off the floor. It came to Letty that Bunny must have some sort of attraction for men imperceptible to her. She asked René, who referred her to Frank. Frank answered at wild cross-purposes. "Yes, yes, of course. She's very feminine. But I'm too old and too busy to take on anything like that."

It gave Letty a new idea about why the suitcases had been entrusted to Bunny. Soon afterwards she asked her if she'd heard from Louis and if he were all right. Bunny beat about the bush a bit, keeping a sharp watch on Letty's face. She must have found the reassurance she sought because, in a rush, she admitted she'd had Poste Restante letters but none recently. He kept on the move so she didn't know where he was, or how. "I only know," she said, "that he won't be coming back for some long time."

Letty had had a happy exchange of letters with John and Laura. Quite early on John had managed to get a letter through begging for news. She had replied with a short condensed account of how things stood and the reason why she had moved into their house. She got an ecstatic answer from Laura. They had long given up hope for the pictures and the house; they only prayed that Letty was safe and well. She couldn't wait to get back, but of course she'd have to; John was tied down at the War Office. Letty did not know how their letters got to her; hers had been carried to England in the pocket of one of her RAF men.

The Allies were deep in Germany now with the Germans surrendering in vast numbers. Then, one day, American and Russian patrols met; the East and West were joined. Surely, this must mean the end? An Admiral Dönitz was acting as head of the German state and had sent envoys to Eisenhower. What had happened to Hitler? Unconditional Surrender was signed by a General Jodl and ratified at Berlin on the night of May 9. Rumor had it that Hitler committed suicide in his bunker; some people believed that he had left the sinking ship for Spain or South America. Letty felt it did not matter; his power was gone, the myth scotched.

Everyone waited for the return of the prisoners. What no one was prepared for were the survivors from the concentration camps. They were whisked away, out of sight, by their families or by special committees formed to look after them.

There were dazzling photographs of prisoners of war embracing their wives or mothers on station platforms, but the ones Letty recognized in the streets of Cannes looked pretty gloomy. The Winslows' gardener came to the house to report for work after he'd been home for a week. Letty took him on at once in John's name. She had known him for years and he talked quite openly to her about his life in Germany and his work there as a farm laborer. They had always had more than enough to eat and good warm clothes. He was still shocked by the conditions in France. His wife and little girl were suffering; they were ill from lack of nourishment. And there was nothing he could do about it. "It's pretty crazy," he said, "to find yourself worse off at home than you were in jail."

"Wonders will never cease, as my old nurse used to say," René announced at dinner one night. "Mary Fowler is back at the Carlton, large as life and fresh as a daisy, with a new entourage in the guise of American colonels. She sent her love," he said to Letty.

Nina made a face and Bunny murmured that she used to know her years ago.

"You'll know her again; the time is ripe for it," he said.

They were silent, thinking of Mary Fowler. René went on; he was wound up. "My shady past is catching up with me. In the last few days I've been approached by mysterious individuals who say they've heard I'm good at forging papers, and would I please make cartes d'identité for them. They flashed their moneybags."

"What did you say?" Nina leaned forward to look at him.

René laughed. "I shouldn't like to repeat it. I threw them out."

After dinner Letty and René went off to John's study for a business conference. René had brought his briefcase which was always a sign. He stacked some bank notes on the desk and placed a paperweight on top. He told her not to put it in the safe yet because, if she agreed, he would draw on it. He settled himself at the desk and motioned Letty into the chair across from him. He began by saying that the prisoners of war were looking for work and that he thought it high time to get on with starting up the brick factory and cement works. He had two men in mind who would make excellent managers. That was essential, the key point. Should he go ahead? They'd choose their own workmen.

Letty agreed; the sooner the better.

"It will take a lot of financing at the beginning."

"Even so," said Letty.

He nodded approval and went over to his briefcase for some papers. "Another matter has come up," he said. "It does not have to be dealt with, but I advise you to do so." He told her that he'd heard from the Syndicate that their clients were back and needed money. They were perfectly aware that the agreement allowed more time. However, if it were not a matter of importance to you, they would be very grateful, etc., etc.

"Everybody," René said, "knows that the franc, in relation to the pound, is pegged at something slightly less than half its true worth. You only have to look at the dollar rate to get that. They all—government officials, businessmen, brokers—predict that the franc-pound exchange will be adjusted within four to six months. *This is the time to pay off your debts*. Remember, I promised francs at the current rate of exchange. If you pay now, you'll save over half!"

"I don't want to cheat them," Letty said, standing up.

"They *need* money; they asked for it."

"In that case, we ought to pay."

"I suggest," he said, "taking out a loan on the Cannes properties we bought."

"A mortgage?" said Letty. "The interest is too high."

"Not when you're doubling your money." He paused to give her time to think.

And think she did; she stood in thought. Then she said, "I can get the money."

"*That much?*" He looked up in astonishment. "It's almost two million."

"Easily," she said. "I'll have it for you tomorrow."

It was René's turn to be silent. Presently he said, "*So you were in on that suitcase business?* The moment we found out who Louis was, we thought it had to be money. We went through the cases; we stripped Bunny's room; we spied on her; we watched everything she did. She didn't move a finger wrong. It was *you* who took the money and stuffed the cases with sheets!"

"I wasn't *in* on anything," said Letty. "I was helping Bunny."

"And what are you doing now?"

"I am helping myself," she said, haughty and complacent. "It doesn't hurt Bunny. She didn't count the money; she never looks at it. I doubt that she ever will, unless Louis turns up."

"And when that happens?" René was staring at her.

"By that time—if it ever does happen—I suppose I shall be rich enough to put it back."

"And if he doesn't come?" René persisted.

"Oh *then!*" said Letty with a shrug. "Bunny is a bit of a goose, you know. She hasn't a clue; she has no idea of what goes on."

"But Louis' money?"

"She won't know the difference. I'll make up the bulk in lower denominations."

René gave a low whistle. "You have come a long way."

"I have," said Letty. "And you won't catch me looking back."